The Unforgettable Leta "Lightning" Laurel

ALSO BY R.L. TOALSON:

The First Magnificent Summer

Something Maybe Magnificent

The Unforgettable Leta "Lightning" Laurel

R.L. TOALSON

ALADDIN
New York   Amsterdam/Antwerp   London
Toronto   Sydney/Melbourne   New Delhi

This book is a work of fiction. Any references to historical events, real people, or real places are used fictitiously. Other names, characters, places, and events are products of the author's imagination, and any resemblance to actual events or places or persons, living or dead, is entirely coincidental.

ALADDIN

An imprint of Simon & Schuster Children's Publishing Division
1230 Avenue of the Americas, New York, New York 10020
For more than 100 years, Simon & Schuster has championed authors and the stories they create. By respecting the copyright of an author's intellectual property, you enable Simon & Schuster and the author to continue publishing exceptional books for years to come. We thank you for supporting the author's copyright by purchasing an authorized edition of this book.
No amount of this book may be reproduced or stored in any format, nor may it be uploaded to any website, database, language-learning model, or other repository, retrieval, or artificial intelligence system without express permission. All rights reserved. Inquiries may be directed to Simon & Schuster, 1230 Avenue of the Americas, New York, NY 10020 or permissions@simonandschuster.com.
First Aladdin hardcover edition May 2025
Text © 2025 by R.L. Toalson
Jacket illustration © 2025 by Dion MBD
All rights reserved, including the right of reproduction in whole or in part in any form.
ALADDIN and related logo are registered trademarks of Simon & Schuster, LLC.
For information about special discounts for bulk purchases, please contact Simon & Schuster Special Sales at 1-866-506-1949 or business@simonandschuster.com.
Simon & Schuster strongly believes in freedom of expression and stands against censorship in all its forms. For more information, visit BooksBelong.com.
The Simon & Schuster Speakers Bureau can bring authors to your live event. For more information or to book an event, contact the Simon & Schuster Speakers Bureau at 1-866-248-3049 or visit our website at www.simonspeakers.com.
Book design by Laura Lyn DiSiena
The text of this book was set in Freight.
Manufactured in the United States of America 0425 BVG
2 4 6 8 10 9 7 5 3 1
Library of Congress Cataloging-in-Publication Data
Names: Toalson, R. L. (Rachel L.), author.
Title: The unforgettable Leta "Lightning" Laurel / by R.L. Toalson.
Description: First Aladdin hardcover edition. | New York : Aladdin, 2025. | Audience term: Preteens | Audience: Ages 8 to 12 | Summary: "A determined girl athlete deals with food insecurity and a new rivalry challenging her feminist ideals."—Provided by publisher.
Identifiers: LCCN 2024040222 (print) | LCCN 2024040223 (ebook) | ISBN 9781665956277 (hc) | ISBN 9781665956291 (ebook)
Subjects: CYAC: Coming of age—Fiction. | Running—Fiction. | Food security—Fiction. | LCGFT: Bildungsromans. | Novels.
Classification: LCC PZ7.1.T587 Un 2025 (print) | LCC PZ7.1.T587 (ebook) | DDC [Fic]—dc23
LC record available at https://lccn.loc.gov/2024040222
LC ebook record available at https://lccn.loc.gov/2024040223

For Mom

I am who I am because you are who you are

Thank you for everything

One

THURSDAY

I don't look like a runner. I look like a rag doll trying to launch myself toward the finish line on rubbery legs that weren't made for this.

But my legs *were* made for this, so I keep going.

The wind blasts against me, picking up for the home stretch. This is about the time my thighs and calves have melted into wobbly blocks of Jell-O, and my arms have numbed completely, my form long gone.

Of course there's a wind when I can't feel my feet.

I just want the misery over.

I chance a look at the sky. Dark clouds glare at me. Storms are pretty typical in April, but . . . is that a tail?

My hearts rams in my throat. I hate tornadoes. I've

never experienced one, and I don't live in a place that sees them often, or, like, ever, but that doesn't stop my brain from whispering, *I think that is a tail. You better run for your life.*

Which makes everything harder. Running for your life is too much pressure. *And* I'm actually running *toward* the possible tail, or the imaginary one, however you want to see it, since it's straight ahead and so is the finish line and the end of my torture.

I can hear Coach Mac yelling from here. The wind's not against her. It snatches her words, twirls them across the football field, and delivers them right to my ears.

"Pick it up, Leta, or I'll add another!"

She'll have to make me crawl another. My legs won't make it through one more four hundred.

I try to pick it up. I really do. But when I cross the finish line and bend over, gasping—just what Coach Mac tells us not to do ("Doesn't let enough air get to your lungs, ladies!" she says)—and Coach Mac calls out my time, I wonder the same thing she asks:

"What's wrong with your feet today, Leta?"

What's wrong with my feet?

I'll tell you what's wrong with my feet: Track shoes are

expensive, which means Mom can't buy a new pair every time mine wear out, which means I run miles and miles in my track shoes, which means all the miles someone else ran in these track shoes before me (because they're not brand-new, they're secondhand, that's the way we have to do things in my family) along with my miles add up to slow slow slow
    SLOW!

Coach Mac has me running the four-hundred-meter dash. It's not quite long enough to wear regular running shoes. It's more of a long-distance sprint, which calls for the special metal-spiked shoes that are supposed to help a runner's toes grip the track so they can run super fast.

    Some of us don't run super fast. At least, not every day. I'd like to remind Coach Mac of that, right now, when she's looking at me like I'm some alien who stole Leta Laurel's body and is now pretending she can run. Sometimes we're tired. Sometimes our feet don't work. Sometimes we have terrible shoes.

    I'm practicing today in my track spikes because our next meet is Saturday. Coach Mac likes us to spend our last practice before our meets in the shoes we'll wear for our race.

    The spikes on track shoes should be sharp. Mine are

so dull you might mistake them for one of those thimbles Mom wears when she's sewing the hem of my pants, which have to be let out every month or so. Every time I bring her another pair for her magical alteration skills, she says, can I please stop growing? I tell her I'd really love to, have you ever been taller than just about every boy *and* girl *and* person *and* teacher in your school? I passed her up by the time I hit fifth grade, so I already know that answer.

Growing is a problem, because Mom just bought me these track shoes six weeks ago and already they feel tight against my toes.

But I won't tell her that. Anything that costs money makes Mom get that anxious look on her face. And I don't like making Mom more anxious than she already is.

When I first handed Mom the track practice schedule, she beamed at me and said, "You made the team!" She looked so happy, I didn't have the heart to tell her everybody made the team. Our school's too small not to take everybody who wants to run track—and even then, Coach Mac isn't above begging more girls to join with promises of monkey bread breakfasts before meets and free pizza on the way home. That's not why I joined, but it's probably why half the girls are on the team. Not a lot of money around these parts, and free pizza is free pizza. And have you ever tried monkey bread?!

When I told Mom Coach Mac assigned me to the four-hundred-meter dash, her face fell like a shot-put ball in the hands of a weakling. Even she knew what kind of shoes you need for any race that ends in "dash."

The most expensive kind.

"Let me see those shoes," Coach Mac says.

I wonder what she'd do if I pretended she wasn't talking to me. But since she'd probably make me run another four hundred and my legs are already fried, I stop and lift up a foot.

"*Give* me the shoe, I mean," Coach Mac says, rolling her eyes.

I almost say, "But it's really stinky," but I decide she gets what she deserves. I pull it off and hand it to her.

She wrinkles her nose before turning it over. She clicks her tongue and shakes her head. "Well, now I see why my star runner can't seem to do more than lumber like a deranged giraffe."

She doesn't mean that. Does she?

A couple of girls giggle. They're no friends of mine. They're girls who can afford the sort of shoes that should make them faster, if they had any kind of running talent.

That's mean. I shouldn't say it. But at least the words

stayed in my thoughts instead of hurtling out of my mouth.

"It's the wind," I mumble. I've never liked running against the wind. Why can't our school build an indoor track?

I know why. It's because all the athletics money goes to football. Surprise, surprise. It's not fair, but it's also not unusual. You pick any school in Texas, and it's the same "football is king" story.

Good spikes would help against the wind. I know this. I stare at the ground.

"Get yourself some new spikes before this weekend's meet," Coach Mac says.

Doesn't she know that's easier said than done? Track spikes aren't in the budget.

Unless Dad magically decides this week is the week he'll start sending Mom some money from his out-of-state job way up in Michigan, which doesn't seem to pay much. But since he hasn't done that in three years, I think it's probably unlikely.

I do believe in miracles. Just not that kind.

"Yes, ma'am," I say anyway. And my chest pinches up tight, which is what happens anytime I think about Dad and the silence and what it might mean.

Coach Mac hands back the shoe, but not before wrinkling her nose again. "And try some baking soda inside." She waves a hand in front of her nose, like she's trying to get rid of something foul. A dead skunk in the middle of the road when it's ninety-nine degrees out and the air conditioner is blasting on high so the dead smell gets caught in the car and you'll never get it out. The fumes from the boys' bathroom at school, which doesn't have a true working door and gifts everyone who passes with an unexpected (but should be expected) whiff. One of Amelia's Spam farts when we're trapped in a car with two windows that don't roll down.

I almost tell Coach Mac the smell was there before I ever wore the shoes in the first place, but that would give away a secret I don't want to tell. I'm just glad she didn't notice the giant layer of superglue I applied to the flapping sole this morning. Which does not seem to work as well as it advertised.

I sigh and wriggle my foot back into the shoe, feeling a little like one of Cinderella's ugly stepsisters.

How's a girl supposed to run in shoes that don't fit, shoes that flap, shoes that can't grip any better than the seal on one of those off-brand sandwich bags Mom has to buy because they're cheaper and we're on a tight budget?

You know how I know about the terrible, no-good, very bad seal of those off-brand sandwich bags Mom has to buy?

Because the day I decided to take a leftover egg salad sandwich to school instead of the usual PB&J was the same day I stuck that sandwich in one of those off-brand sandwich bags and straight into my backpack instead of my lunch bag.

There's a reason I left my lunch bag at home. I got tired of bringing my old rainbow unicorn lunch bag from fourth grade, when I'm in eighth grade. I mean, I still love rainbows and I sleep with a stuffed unicorn, but those are things people don't have to see. You know?

I decided to take matters into my own hands and use my backpack as a lunch bag.

Sometimes you make terrible decisions you wish you could take back. This was one of them.

Anyway. I zipped the bag closed. But it didn't stay zipped closed.

Oh no.

By the time lunch rolled around, egg salad had smashed into every crevice of the only new thing I got to kick off my eighth-grade year: a purple backpack.

And you know what? The bad day didn't end there. Of course it didn't. It followed me home.

I tried to wash my backpack free of its egg salad, but the only thing I washed it free of was its perfect purple color.

Now I walk around with a backpack that's more pale lavender than perfect purple. Turns out backpacks on the clearance rack aren't made to be washed.

There's another reason I might be slow that has nothing to do with my track shoes, but I don't like to think about it.

Puberty.

Coach Mac starts every track season talking to us about puberty. I've heard her speech two years in a row, so I practically have it memorized.

"Young women throughout history have gone through puberty, and that means changing bodies," she tells us. "And sometimes it also means slower run times for a while, until you get used to your new, changing bodies." She squints at us during this part, like she's trying to see which ones of us will believe her and which ones won't. I don't know if she can actually tell, but I always try to make my face say I believe everything she says. Because I do. She's one of the smartest people I know, besides Mom and Pop.

"Your bodies, however they look during the changing, do not tell the future of your running career," she also tells us. "Things will settle into their proper places, and you'll find your stride again."

I think she might have been talking about boobs when she said, "Things will settle into their proper places." They throw off your whole center of gravity for a while. I've heard.

Coach Mac also regularly tells us things like "Don't worry about your weight, girls. Make sure you're eating enough food to fuel your body. Do not EVER stop eating because you think lighter is faster. It's not. It's a myth, and my girls are too smart to fall for myths."

She's very passionate about that.

She's very passionate about every part of running, actually. She's the only coach I know who buys sports bras for anyone who needs them. "No person should be excluded from track just because her family can't afford a good sports bra," she says. I've taken a couple from her, since I know Mom doesn't have the money for expensive sports bras, only the cheap ones that need constant adjusting. Who wants to adjust a bra while they're running in front of other people?

Track shoes and track spikes aren't included in the community treasure chest, though, so we're on our own for those. Track shoes are too expensive for Coach Mac to give away. But I'm not sure why she hasn't thought of the cost of track spikes. Maybe because they're not *that* expensive for most people. Or because we don't need to replace them often—most of my teammates are still wearing the same ones they wore last season; mine just came old, so they're already close to stubs.

Or maybe it's because I've never mentioned I need help getting them.

I don't mention it because it's kind of embarrassing. No one wants to admit their family can't afford new track spikes. When you admit you can't afford ten extra dollars, people look at you a certain kind of way. I learned that back in third grade, when I told my teacher I didn't have a fold-out poster board for our wax museum project because my mom had to buy groceries that week. Some kid said, "My poster board only cost two dollars," like that made a difference. Two dollars will also buy two bags of beans.

Anyway. Back to puberty. Why does it always have to come back to puberty?

Coach Mac used to be a professional runner, so she also starts every season teaching us how to monitor our periods. She hands us all a pocket-size calendar and says, "Look, girls, no one talked to me about this when I was your age. But it's important to know where you are in your cycle and adjust your training to best suit your body. Your period is your business, and I would never, ever share that information with anyone else. But I'm here to help anytime you need it."

If we don't want to track our period, she says that's our choice and our business too.

"Not everyone has predictable cycles, especially in the beginning," Coach Mac says. "But they can be important indicators of your running health."

What she means is, we can monitor our periods to make sure we're not getting into what she called RED-S.

"It's a condition we don't want to play around with," she tells us as often as possible. "I saw far too many of my colleagues end their careers too early because of it."

Basically, she says if we start our periods and they're pretty regular and then we run a lot and get too thin because of the running and then go months and months where we don't have a period, it can sometimes—but not always—mean we're not eating enough to run as much as we run. And that can lead to holes in our bones, which makes them easier to break.

I think she told us that last part to scare us a little. And it works—at least for me!

Coach Mac isn't just making all this up, either. I googled it, and RED-S is a real thing. It can end running careers, just like she said.

Being a girl is complicated.

So I monitor my period every month. So does everyone else, I think. And if we need to talk to Coach Mac about something, she takes us into her office, closes her door, and lets us ask our questions, however personal or ridiculous, and she never tells another person. It's like having a big sister or another mom or a friend who's a little bit scary sometimes.

I don't think there are many coaches like her, but I'm pretty sure there should be more.

Although, she's not perfect. She once told me, in the middle of practice, while the boys jogged past, "I got another sports bra for you to try, Leta. I found a smaller size."

I ran super fast that day, trying to outrun my burning face.

I still took the bra.

Two

THURSDAY

Chrissy Amaro and Raina Vincent walk next to me on the way to the bus. The other friend in our four-person BFF group, Sabrina Billings, is still over at the long jump. But she doesn't ride the bus anyway. Her mom is already waiting for her in the parking lot.

And she hasn't been hanging out with us recently. I don't know why. I don't like to think about it. It makes my chest squeeze in a really uncomfortable way.

"Those four hundreds are no joke," Chrissy says. "I thought my legs were gonna fall off." She runs the mile, and she does not like to sprint.

"That's how I feel every race," I say.

"That sounds like the worst race ever," Chrissy says. "I'd rather pace myself."

"And the lungs," Raina says. "How do they burn so much without exploding? Do you think I have a tear? Will I even be able to run this meet?" Raina runs the two hundred. She doesn't like distances longer than that, even though she runs the mile relay with me and Chrissy and Sabrina. She has short legs that blur into wheels when she's running. It's impressive.

Chrissy snorts. "I don't think you can tear a lung from running."

"You'd be surprised," Raina says. She rubs her chest. "I don't know how you do it, Leta."

"Well, I didn't really do it today," I say.

Chrissy waves a hand. "Coach is just being Coach," she says.

I hope.

"I tried to imagine a tornado was coming to get me," I say. Chrissy snorts again. "But even that didn't work. My legs just wouldn't cooperate."

"Maybe you're getting close to your period," Raina says. Coach Mac says the week leading up to our periods increases inflammation, which can make us feel like we're running slower, even if we actually aren't.

I haven't checked my calendar in a while. Maybe Raina's right.

I don't really know what happens next. One minute I'm walking with Raina and Chrissy, the next I'm on the ground.

"Whoa," Chrissy says. "You okay, Leta?"

Uh. No. Everything hurts. But I say, "Yeah, I'm fine."

Chrissy sticks out her hand and helps me up. "You gotta pick up your feet when you're walking over a curb," she says. She's trying not to laugh. And even though my knee stings and I can see a little pebble stuck in it, I try not to laugh too.

I'm graceful on the track, but not so graceful off it.

Our bus driver, Mr. Meinke, honks twice. He squints at us. He wants to get this over and done with, deliver us to our homes so he's free to enjoy the rest of his evening.

"Whoops," Chrissy says. "Guess we're taking too long."

"Lollygagging," Raina says, which makes us all laugh. It's Mr. Meinke's favorite word to describe what we're doing.

We hurry toward the bus. None of us wants to miss it, because it's our only ride home.

Raina makes a sour face in the direction of Sabrina's mom. "I wonder what it's like, having a mom show up for everything. Even practices."

Raina can ask a question like this because she lives with her grandma and grandpa. Her mom's long gone, someplace no one knows. Her dad's a bank manager or something two towns away. He sends her a card and some money on her birthday every year. She never sees him except for two weeks every summer.

If I asked the question, it would feel like a betrayal. Mom's doing the best she can. No sense in wishing she could do better.

But my throat starts throbbing anyway.

Because what would it be like not to feel like so much of your life had to be spent alone?

Don't get me wrong. I know Mom has to work her two jobs so she can take care of me and my sister, Amelia. I'm not mad about it.

At least not most days.

(Usually the days she comes home with mushy fruit she has to clear out of the displays at the grocery store down the road, which she makes into jam. We always have the best jam.)

Amelia and I have gone home to an empty house since my first day of fourth grade. Amelia was in kindergarten.

I tell you what, a nine-year-old grows up faster than I can run a four hundred when she has to take care of a five-year-old, especially a five-year-old like Amelia. It's a split-second growing-up. You don't want to know how many times I had to go get Amelia from the backyard when

I turned away for a second to put the fish sticks and french fries—our supper—into the oven. You don't want to know what kinds of threats I had to make so she'd stay put. And you really don't want to know how many times I lost her, how many hours I spent searching the streets for an expert escape artist, or how much I wished I didn't have to look after my annoying little sister.

I'm pretty sure Amelia's the reason I have anxiety.

None of that is Mom's fault. It's just the way things have to be. Sometimes you have to grow up and help out where you can and try to make things easier for your mom, who never ever gets to put her feet up and rest.

At least those days of chasing Amelia and making sure she doesn't die are over. Mostly.

Amelia's in fourth grade now, which means she's perfectly fine staying home alone until either Mom gets home (on Wednesdays) or Pop and I get home (on Mondays, Tuesdays, and Thursdays). She has me on Fridays since I don't ever have track practice the day before a meet.

But if I'm being honest, I still worry about her. If she couldn't do what she was supposed to while I was watching her, how does she do what she's supposed to when no one's eyes can see?

I just tell myself I'm not her mom, and some days that works.

Raina's stop is the first one. A pile of kids gets off at her corner, mostly boys who shove each other down the stairs. I wince, watching them, hoping they don't shove Raina down with them.

She's really small.

But she appears a second later and waves. "See you tomorrow!"

Chrissy hangs out the window until Mr. Meinke tells her, "Get your head back inside the bus, young lady."

He has a very serious face with a very serious white mustache and the kind of eyebrows that look like they're waving at you. But not to be friendly. To make you go away, more like it.

Chrissy waves a hand out the window instead. I think Mr. Meinke is glad the next stop is hers.

The trailers in Harmony Park look dingy and sad, except for Chrissy's trailer at the end. It's the brightest thing here, painted the kind of blue that looks like a summer sky in the late afternoon.

"See you tomorrow!" Chrissy calls as she heads toward the exit.

I wave back and say, "Don't forget to bring a lunch this time!"

Chrissy gives me a thumbs-up.

Her mom makes the best tortillas and sends about a dozen to school every day. And since I don't get lunch anymore, Chrissy tries to pawn off her extras on me.

I don't mind as much as you'd think—not just because Chrissy's mom makes the best tortillas, but because there's a reason I stopped eating lunch.

It's not what you think.

Some girls stop eating lunch because they think they need to be thin and that's the way to do it. I've heard them talk about calories and all those tips they read in magazines—blotting the grease off pizza, a handful of almonds instead of a handful of chips, drinking a full glass of water before a meal so you don't eat as much.

But that's not why I stopped eating lunch.

I stopped eating lunch because when you're on the free lunch program, or the one that says you only have to pay fifty cents instead of two dollars and twenty-five cents, certain people look at you like you matter about as much as the discarded toenails they clipped before coming to track practice so they could avoid toenail trauma. It's not like they announce these things or something. Everything's digital, so no one has to know. We go through the line like everybody else. But kids seem to know which ones of us get free lunches somehow. Maybe it's the way we look or the clothes we wear. I don't know.

They whisper things they've heard from their parents: "Did you hear she doesn't pay for lunch? I hate people who take advantage of the system." "Wish I got a free lunch like some people." "So poor she has a cell phone."

I don't have a cell phone. Only Mom has one, because they're expensive.

It's hard not to feel like something's wrong with you when you hear things like that.

I guess I got tired of hearing the talk, feeling their stares, knowing they were judging me for something I had no control over. So I stopped standing in the lunch line. And since we hardly ever have enough leftover food to pack my own lunch, I decided skipping lunch was a good solution all around. It's easier to pretend I'm not hungry.

No one reports to Mom whether or not I eat lunch, so she never even has to know, which means she doesn't have to feel more guilty or anxious about our situation—which is not her fault, either—than she already does.

I'm hungry all the time.

I'm a runner.

What do you expect?

Three

THURSDAY

Mondays, Tuesdays, and Thursdays are my favorite days, because Pop's the one who picks me up at the bus stop. Mom's usually late, and I spend ten whole minutes trying to calm my anxiety and wipe away all the gruesome images my mind volunteers to answer the question, *Why is she late this time?* Usually my helpful brain says, *Well, she's probably dead, and here's how.*

Pop's never late, because he's the best grandpa ever. He's already waiting at the post office, which is my stop because we live out in the middle of nowhere. I can see Amelia slumped in the back seat.

Pop jumps out of the car the minute he sees me walk down the steps of the bus.

"Leta!" he says before springing toward me like he's not sixty-five years old.

Mom says I got my running legs from Pop. And he's sure proud of them. His short shorts show his pasty white limbs like they're his crowning glory. They're almost the same color as the post office door behind him.

Do my legs look that white and pasty? I hope not.

I check over my shoulder to make sure the bus is already on its way. Even though it is, I'm about 99 percent certain everyone still on the bus has seen Pop and his legs.

Oh well. It's not like everybody in this town and Francitas and the other two towns around us haven't seen him out in short shorts just about every day, racing himself down miles and miles of highway.

Pop still runs. When I'm not embarrassed about it, I think it's the coolest thing ever.

Pop taps the steering wheel. "How many four hundreds today, Speedy?"

Pop likes to tease me with nicknames like Speedy, La Rápida, Bolt. I don't mind so much, as long as he doesn't do it in front of my friends.

He's coming to my track meet Saturday. There's no telling what he'll do there. Pop's kind of a wild card—the kind who gets thrown off a small-town golf course for stealing clubs from the players and taking off running, laughing manically (it was just a joke, he said later); who breaks out into a dance in the grocery store parking lot when a passing car's stereo blasts "Dance Monkey"; who takes his friends at the old folks' home on wild rides through town on his golf cart.

He's like a kid trapped in a sixty-five-year-old body.

"Earth to Bolt," Pop says. He makes a crackling noise like it's static on a radio.

I forgot to answer his question. Sometimes I do that. I get stuck in my head. My own world, Mom calls it. My own world is such an interesting place because it doesn't have all the questions this one does, like *Why did Dad leave? Why is he still gone? When will he come home? What if he never does?*

"Ten," I say.

"Ten," he says. He whistles. "You hear that, Amelia? Your sister ran almost three miles today." He grins at me.

Amelia doesn't say anything, just glares out the back seat window. She probably didn't want to come. But the last time Pop left her home alone on a Monday, Tuesday, or Thursday, she ate seven iffy oranges (Mom was planning to use them in some jam) and a whole two pounds of fresh red grapes that should have lasted a week. Mom just about flipped out, but it was nothing compared to Amelia's stomach later that night.

"How many did you run?" I say.

Pop shrugs. "It was an easy day."

I wait. He'll tell me if I wait long enough. He can't help it. If there's anything Pop loves as much as running, it's talking about running.

Just before we turn onto my street, Pop says, "Nineteen."

He's not talking about four hundreds. He's talking about miles.

Sheesh. Shown up by my sixty-five-year-old grandpa. What am I doing with my life?

Pop digs around in the refrigerator, pulls out two oranges and some old carrots. "Nothing to eat in here," he says. "How do you power those legs?"

I shrug.

Pop glides over to the pantry, moves some things around. "Nothing here, either."

He looks at me, then Amelia, then me, then Amelia. "I guess we'll just have to go into town and get some chicken."

"Yes!" Amelia says. She practically jumps in the air. Amelia loves Kentucky Fried Chicken, one of five restaurants in town, along with a Sonic, the McDonald's, a barbecue place that caters pretty much every wedding in the county, and a Mexican food place that serves nacho cheese instead of salsa. Pop eats lunch there with his friends every Tuesday. He says it gives him the runs. And he's not talking about miles.

    Sometimes he has a problem oversharing.

    "Let's go!" Pop says, shaking a fist in the air.

    I don't know why, but my stomach twists a little.

    Maybe I'm starting to believe what some of the girls on the team whisper when Coach Mac's not around.

What some of the girls on the team whisper:

    "Eat too much fried chicken, pizza, hamburgers—any kind of food, really—and you gain weight."

    "Gain too much weight and you won't have a chance at winning a race."

    "If you can't win a race, you don't belong on the team. You're nothing."

    Is winning and belonging on a team, being something, only available to small, skinny people who don't eat too much fried chicken?

Four

THURSDAY

"What's wrong with you, Leta?" Pop says, eyeing my full plate. I've been picking at everything except the green beans.

We ordered the chicken and brought it home—which is much better than eating it there. There has eyes. And people who might know you. And see you in your sweaty track shorts. And whisper about you in the halls tomorrow.

Junior high wasn't supposed to be this hard. But it seems like there are so many unspoken rules for girls that I never knew about before. Don't be too smart. Don't boss boys around. Don't wear anything that might distract the boys. Don't argue. Don't show off. Don't be selfish. Don't challenge the way things are, even if they're not fair.

Most of the girls in my school see *everything* as a competition. None of us know what the prize is.

It's all very confusing and exhausting, and when I let myself think about it long enough, I want to punch a hole in the sky. Or, as Mom would say, the box that's trying to keep me small. Keep *us* small. We're all trying to break out of it, I guess.

I didn't know there was a box until I got to junior high. I glance at Amelia. She has one more year of innocence.

I spear some green beans (probably a little too hard) and shove them into my mouth. I'm practically starving, but...

Pop set aside a plate for Mom. It waits for her in the refrigerator. She won't eat it. She'll try to give it to me or Amelia.

"Aren't you hungry after all those four hundreds?" Pop says.

I shrug. "Not really."

It's torture lying to him. It's also torture smelling this chicken. I want to eat every bit of it on my plate. But I tear off one piece from a chicken breast—white meat has fewer calories, I think—and tell myself that's it. That's all I'm having.

"Dark meat's what's good for runners," Pop says. He bites into his fifth piece at least. He can spare the calories. He ran *nineteen miles*.

But okay, one more bite. I tear off a piece from the thigh this time.

Mom's tires pop on the gravel out front, and I take that moment to shove my plate away with an "I'll save the rest for later." Like Mom does.

Pop looks at me for too long, like he knows exactly what I'm doing even when I don't have a clue.

Mom looks tired when she walks through the door. She hates her second job, but she says we need the money for gas and electricity and rising grocery costs.

I eye my dull track shoes in the corner of the kitchen. Maybe I'll ask her about new spikes later, or maybe I'll just do my best with what I have. It's not a super-important meet. Just another one to see what we're made of.

"Hello, girls. Dad." Mom sets down her purse, bends and kisses the top of Amelia's head, and blows a kiss at me. "I know you haven't showered," she says.

I try not to take offense. Do I really smell that bad?

Not to myself.

Pop says, "We picked up some food in town."

And that look crosses Mom's face, even if it's only for a split second. The worried look. The one that says, *More fast food?*

But for the life of me, I can't figure out if she's worried about fast food because of Pop, me and Amelia, or herself.

Maybe it's all of us.

I watch Mom take a piece of chicken and dish out a tiny dot of mashed potatoes and some green beans.

She picks at her food like me. Pop watches her too.

I still feel his eyes on me every now and then. I really want to finish those mashed potatoes. And the chicken, too. I should put them away so I'm not tempted to.

No one says anything until Pop says, "How was work?"

"Same old story," Mom says.

You'd think being a fruit stocker at the local grocery store would be an easy job, but you'd be surprised how touchy people get about their fruit. Mom's been yelled at for bruised peaches and watermelons moved to the corner of the store instead of the center. She says she doesn't care, it's not personal, but how's a person stop caring when someone insults you?

I wish I could learn that trick.

She loves her job at the school, though. She only finished one semester of college before she dropped out to marry Dad, but she's in line to become the elementary school librarian anyway when old Mrs. Sutton retires this year.

Mom will be a good librarian. She reads in voices and plays with puppets and organizes book fairs.

"How was your day?" Mom throws out the question to everybody, but Pop's the only one who answers.

"Slow and steady," he says.

I'm not sure if he's talking about the nineteen miles he ran today or his job.

Pop hasn't retired because he runs his own air-conditioning-repair business. He doesn't do much anymore, just oversees everything. But he's still important in the eyes of his workers. They all stand a little straighter when he walks through the doors. I've seen it.

Pop's real good at that: making people stand a little bit straighter.

He wasn't always good at making people stand a little bit straighter. He has a history of mistakes. He left my nana when Mom was just a little girl, and it took him a long time to come back.

But I guess the important thing is he came back.

Pop stays for a while after supper. Amelia and I disappear to our room.

I had really hoped, when we moved here, that I'd get my own room, but it turns out I'll be sharing a room with Amelia until I leave or I die, whichever comes first.

Some days it gets on my nerves, but most days I don't mind so much.

We don't turn on any music or even talk when we get to our room, so even though Mom's and Pop's voices are quiet, we hear everything.

Pop starts to say, "If you need a hand, you know—"

"I don't need anything from you." Mom sounds mad. Or maybe sad. Sometimes it's hard to tell.

"Sometimes we fall on hard times," Pop says. "Need a little help getting back on our feet."

"We're doing fine," Mom says.

But are we? Mom doesn't get paid for another week at least, and the pantry and refrigerator are almost empty.

"Okay," Pop says. His voice definitely sounds sad. I blink hard. "Any word from—"

"No." Mom sighs. "I don't really expect to hear anything at this point. He tends to forget he has kids who need him."

How's a person forget a thing like that? I look at Amelia. She plays with a loose thread on the bedspread. I want to tell her, "Dad didn't forget us," but I don't know if I believe it now that Mom's said the words out loud. Maybe we're just forgettable.

"He's their father," Pop says.

"Yeah, well, dads don't always stick around. Or remember birthdays. Or send money."

The room falls so quiet they can probably hear me and Amelia breathing, listening in.

"I'm sorry, Dad," Mom finally says. "I'm just . . . a little stressed is all."

Mom used to think Pop didn't remember her birthday or send money or want to stick around. But it turns out my nana hid a lot of things from Mom, including that Pop sent birthday cards with money every year and called to talk and asked to see Mom all the time.

Mom's not doing that with Dad's cards or letters or phone calls. He doesn't write or call. Ever.

Pop doesn't say anything. The chairs squeal like they're getting up. The front door opens. Pop says, "There are programs that can help, you know."

"I don't need any programs," Mom says. "We'll be okay."

I try as hard as I can to believe her.

Because I share a room with Amelia, Mom makes me go to bed at 8:15, the same time Amelia has to go to bed. Some nights I try to fight it.

Tonight I guess I'm just tired.

We say the same thing we always do.

"Good night, Amelia."

"Good night, Leta."

"Sweet dreams."

"Sweet dreams."

"See you in the morning."

"Okay. See you in the morning."

"Okay. Love you."

"Love you, too."

I listen to Amelia's breathing get deeper and thicker before turning over and staring out our window.

Two months ago, Amelia stared out this same window, when the stars looked close enough to touch, and she said, "I wish Dad would come home for my daddy-daughter dance."

The daddy-daughter dance that's now four weeks away.

Why do people even have daddy-daughter dances? Don't they know some daughters don't have daddies?

That night I made a wish too. I wished that I could figure out a way to make Amelia's wish come true. It sounded more like a promise than a wish. I would find a way. For Amelia.

The moon is almost all the way full. I stare at it until the darkness of night falls away and all I can see is a round split of light.

So when I close my eyes, it never leaves me.

Five

FRIDAY

Mom wakes us up before leaving for her job at the elementary school six miles away.

"Make sure your sister gets on the bus," she says before kissing my head and disappearing out the door with a "Have a great day!"

Mom used to take Amelia with her to school, since they both go to the same place, but Amelia hates getting there so early, and I think she probably makes Mom's job harder. So now Amelia rides the bus with me. The bus stops at the elementary school before heading to the junior high. Not enough kids live out here to justify two buses.

So now it's my responsibility to make sure Amelia

gets out to the bus stop at the end of our driveway on time and with everything she needs.

I try to. I really do.

But Amelia has a bad habit of going into our closet like she's looking for some clothes and falling back asleep right there on the floor!

This morning, after the third time I've caught her snoozing, I don't leave her side for a second. Which means I don't get to fix my hair and have to pull it up in a quick ponytail, which makes me grumpy because the one day a week I don't have track practice and we don't do anything much in athletics class but sit around because Coach Mac is superstitious and thinks making her runners run around the day before a track meet is sure to invite bad luck, I'd really like to fix my hair.

"Come on, Amelia," I growl. I help her zip up her backpack around a folder and more books than a fourth grader has any business carrying. (They're probably overdue library books she never got around to reading. Amelia hardly ever reads. Ironic, since Mom's an assistant librarian and all.) "We gotta go!"

The bus will show up any second. If Amelia's not on it, Mom will be furious.

Sometimes I wish I were an only child. You know how

much easier life would be if I only had to worry about myself?

I swear my sister moves like a sloth. If I moved that slow, I'd get lapped trying to finish a four hundred.

I grab two oranges from the refrigerator and toss one to Amelia.

"Come on, come on, come on!"

"I don't like oranges," Amelia says.

"Since when?"

"Since forever?"

Amelia's giving me sass. She ate oranges, like, three days ago. "Fine," I say. I hold up an apple, the last one in the drawer. It has a couple of bruises. Amelia wrinkles her nose and shakes her head. I let my frustration loose in a loud breath. I point to a very brown banana on the counter.

Amelia shakes her head again.

"What, then?"

She marches over to the pantry and pulls out a dusty can of Spam.

Gross. I don't even think Mom meant to buy that. She may not have. It may have been a donation. Sometimes we get those.

But there's no time to argue with Amelia about nutritious food and good choices. I can hear the brakes of the bus at the stop before ours.

"Go, go, go!" I say.

But something catches my eye on the table. The local newspaper. The front page has a picture of two kids grinning at the camera, each holding a trophy for some math competition.

And I suddenly get the best idea I've had in a long time.

If Dad tends to forget he has kids who need him, all we have to do is remind him we're here.

All *I* have to do is win the four-hundred-meter race at district. They'll put my picture in the paper, and Mom will send a clipping to Dad. He'll see it and think, *That's right. Leta and Amelia, my daughters, who need me.*

Then he'll come back home.

Just in time for Amelia's daddy-daughter dance.

"Bus!"

Amelia's voice drags me out the door so fast I almost forget to lock it. Not that we really need to lock the front door way out here in the middle of nowhere. I always do it anyway. You never know what kind of trouble can find you, even in the safest places.

Mom says that's part of being a woman. She had a talk with me the summer before sixth grade. She called it the Things You Need to Know About Being a Woman Talk.

It was much more than I bargained for.

Amelia and I sprint down the gravel driveway. Mrs. Malcolm, our morning bus driver, waits for us. As long as she can see us coming, she waits.

Even with the windows down, everybody knows when Amelia opens her can of Spam.

"Ew! What is that smell?!" Nicole Stanley says. "It smells like someone's sewage system backed up!"

We actually do smell that a lot on our way to school. People don't have very strong sewage systems out here.

"Smells like the boys' locker room," one of the Hamill twins says. They're both pretty good football players, big enough to take down a whole line. It makes them think a lot of themselves, though. They're not very nice.

"Smells like a fish crawled up on land seven days ago and died next to a road-killed deer that's been baking in the sun for three days," says Ryan Hensley.

That's . . . specific.

I put my head down and pretend I don't have a sister.

What Mom Said in Our "Things You Need to Know About Being a Woman" Talk

1. "Don't walk alone at night."
2. "Choose busy places instead of empty ones if you're out by yourself."
3. "Always pay attention. Don't wear two earbuds in public. Don't get lost on your phone in public. I know you don't have either of those things now. But someday you will. And you don't have the luxury of not paying attention."
4. "Your period will come soon. It's natural, and while you might feel afraid of it for a while, you should never feel ashamed of it."
5. "A girl can do anything a boy can do. It's important you don't forget that, no matter what the world tells you."
6. "You are your own brilliant, strong, capable, ambitious self. And don't ever hide that because someone says you should."
7. "Big boobs are overrated."

Six

FRIDAY

Before the first bell rings, no one's allowed in the school building, but since there's nowhere else to go, we just hang out in the yard at the front entrance. Some kids gather in the soccer field across the street, tossing a baseball or actually playing soccer.

I don't like to get all sweaty before school starts.

It's a good thing I didn't get a chance to fix my hair this morning. Amelia's open can of Spam forced everybody to roll down their windows in a desperate attempt to air out the smell, and if my hair hadn't been in a ponytail, it would be a tangled mess right now.

The smell disappeared once Amelia got off the bus. So that made the Hamill twins say a few things I'd rather forget. They don't matter. They're just stupid, rude boys.

Chrissy and Raina are waiting for me in our usual place: in the shade of a great big oak tree. "I brought you some tortillas!" Chrissy says, tossing a foil-wrapped cylinder at me.

I don't have the heart to tell her I won't be eating those tortillas I asked for yesterday. If you want to be fast, you have to be careful what you put in your body. Pop's always saying that. Or . . . something like it, anyway.

And since I want to not just run the four hundred but win the whole thing at district, it's time to get a lot pickier about my fuel, starting today.

"Thanks," I say, and shove the cylinder in my backpack.

Maybe just one tortilla.

Her mom really does make the best.

I'll save it for lunch, I guess.

But when lunch rolls around, I've changed my mind.

Part of it is the rumors.

There's a new girl in the eighth grade. Small, short legs, dark brown hair, dark brown eyes that don't always look in the same place at the same time.

Her name is Natalie Dash. She comes from the town of Yoakum, which has the best track team in the district. I know because Coach Mac is always talking about them.

She calls them our greatest competitors. And she's serious about these things.

Kids are saying Natalie Dash is really fast.

They're saying she's joining the track team.

They're saying her race is the four hundred.

Every meet I run at least two four hundreds—one for the actual race (more if I make it to the final heat, which I always do), one for the mile relay. I'm the anchor on the relay team, the one Coach Mac puts at the end to clinch the win.

Faster, fast, fast, fastest. That's how the lineup goes.

All season, I've been the anchor. All season, I've run the fastest four hundred in the eighth grade.

I'm not about to stop now—especially since there's so much on the line.

Dad has to remember who we are.

I can't let Amelia down.

Doesn't the universe see that?

"You hear what they're all saying?" Raina says. We sit on one side of the picnic table under the shade of another big oak tree, this one in the field between the lunchroom and the band hall. Sabrina and Chrissy sit on the other side.

"Yeah," I say, trying not to think about those foil-wrapped tortillas somewhere in the bottom of my backpack. They're probably smushed beyond recognition now, anyway. They wouldn't even be good. Probably.

My stomach rumbles.

We all look at the new girl, sitting alone on another bench at the corner of the yard, this one near the back of the school and in full sun. No one sits there because it's too hot. She doesn't seem to notice what's going on around her, since a book hides her face.

"She's won every four hundred she's run," Sabrina says. I feel her eyes on me.

I don't look at her, afraid I'll see that little sliver of satisfaction on her face like I saw yesterday at practice when Coach Mac commented on my shoes.

Maybe I just imagined it. We formed our best friend group in the third grade. But Sabrina's been my best friend since kindergarten, when we were both the only five-year-olds to make it all the way across the monkey bars in P.E. without falling.

"You can't believe everything people say," Raina says.

"You can't even believe *half* of what most people say," Chrissy says. "Besides, she's never run against Leta."

I'm so grateful for their words, I want to hug them. And I'm not really a hugger.

Sabrina doesn't say anything. I try to tell myself she's just worried about her place on the mile-relay team. All season, it's been the four of us: Chrissy, leg one; Raina, leg two; Sabrina, leg three; and me, the anchor.

She's the slowest leg on the team.

But I have a feeling it's more than that.

Her name sounds like a running superstar's: "Natalie Dash."

"What can you expect from a person with the last name 'Dash'?" says Quentin Pierce, the cutest boy in the eighth grade (according to Sabrina), during Life Science. "Speed."

"It's like she owns the four hundred," says Ryan Hensley, Quentin's best friend.

He whispers the words, but even sitting three seats away, I can hear them.

I know Natalie, sitting at the lab table right behind him, can hear too.

I sneak a look at her. She studies the book open beside the tray holding a starfish we're supposed to dissect. She doesn't look up.

As far as I know, she's said hardly a word to anyone all day. She ate lunch alone, she walks to class alone, she even sits as far as possible from her lab partner, Trey Navarro, like she prefers to be alone.

"Looks like you've got some competition, Leta." Weston Garner leans over just to tell me that. His whisper's louder than Quentin's and Ryan's.

"Shut up, Weston." I hiss his name, because you can do that with *S*'s.

I feel the new girl's eyes on me, but I don't meet them.

I know it's ridiculous to hate someone you don't even know, but it's much harder not to than you'd think.

My stomach twists, and it has nothing to do with the starfish that smells like it's been dead six months already.

Seven

FRIDAY

The bus ride home is so hot and sweaty, Benny Dunlap, who lives exactly half a mile down the road from my house, walks down the aisle, sliding down the windows on seats where people aren't sitting. He smiles at me when he passes. Something in my stomach does a cartwheel. I think it's that tortilla I ate. I did cave and eat one. And it was not smushed beyond recognition. It was very, very good. But I think it's formed itself into a dough-person, like the Pillsbury Doughboy. He's trapped in my insides, cartwheeling and waving right now.

Outside smells like just-watered grass. I stare out my window, watching cornfields pass. Birds line up on power lines, erupting into black clouds when we pass. Mrs.

Malcolm takes every curve like she's racing someone, and I start to wonder if the school bus will drop right over on its side on every next turn.

We're seven stops away from home when someone says, "Ew! Look at that old man!"

And I know. I KNOW who they're talking about.

I tell myself not to look.

But when we pass the country road right before ours, there he is, in his short-shorts splendor.

Fluorescent orange shirt stuck to his torso, because of course he's all sweaty, running this time of day. Tiny gray shorts showing just about every inch of his skinny legs. Bright red shoes kicking up dust.

I guess I should be glad he's at least wearing a shirt this time.

But why isn't he at work? Or golfing with his friends at the old folks' home? Or . . . doing anything but running roads he knows our bus will take to get home?

He waves so hard when we pass, I wonder if he'll have the energy to finish his run.

But he doesn't stop there.

Of course he doesn't.

"Amelia!" he says. "Leta!" He waves. "I'll race you home!"

I swear Mrs. Malcolm slows down just so he has a fighting chance.

And when we stop for the Hamill twins and the girl at the end of the road, Pop passes us and does a little jig and keeps right on going.

We follow him the rest of the way home.

The first thing I always do as soon as I get home is check the mail. You never know if this will be the day Dad decides to send a letter or some money. Or a card just to say, *I do remember you.*

The next thing I always do is check the answering machine. You never know if this will be the day Dad decides to call, leave a good number where we can reach him (the only number we have was disconnected four months ago), say the words I know he's been meaning to say: "How could I ever forget a daughter as awesome as you?"

The third thing I always do is get a snack from the fridge, but since there isn't much there and the answering machine has no new message and the only thing that waits in the mailbox is a spider with a web that swallows the entire back half of it and three egg sacs arranged in a triangle, I don't feel much like eating anyway.

Amelia grabs the last dusty can of Spam in the pantry and makes the whole house smell like the bus did earlier today. I didn't realize there were two cans. Maybe Mom did buy them on purpose.

"You're gonna rot your insides," I say. Two cans of Spam in one day seems like a very bad decision.

Amelia flashes me a grin, complete with half-chewed Spam peeking out. She laughs and nearly sprays it at me.

I sigh and plop down on the chair that used to be Dad's. It folds around me, like a warm, gentle hug Dad could never seem to give.

I close my eyes.

"Got something for you," Pop says.

I guess I dozed a little in Dad's old chair. Pop stands in the doorway, looking at me. "I need your track shoes, though."

"Why?"

"You'll see." He sits on the couch. "Just get your shoes."

I eye the doorway. If I get up, Amelia might steal the chair. But I can't ask Pop to get my shoes. He's old, and besides, who knows how many miles he ran to get here? He still has to run back home, which is six more miles away!

I check the room and the kitchen one more time. Maybe Amelia went outside to play with her two friends who live at the end of our gravel driveway, which she's not supposed to do unless Mom is home. She doesn't care. Amelia does what she wants.

The coast looks clear, so I race to my room, grab my track shoes from my gym bag, and race back out.

Amelia rocks in Dad's chair, a smirk on her mean little face.

I almost throw a shoe at her, but I'll have to wait until Pop's gone. He probably won't think it's justified.

"Whew!" Pop says. "These shoes smell terrible!"

"They were like that before I got them," I grumble.

I don't know if he heard me. He turns the one I gave him over, runs a hand over the spikes. "How do you spring in these with spikes this dull?" He furrows his eyebrows at me.

I shrug. I don't tell him it doesn't matter how sharp your spikes are when your sole flaps on the left foot. Toes can't grab the track with a flapping sole.

I gave him the right shoe. I'm still holding the left one.

I just hope he doesn't notice the flapping sole. He'll feel sorry for me, and I hate when people feel sorry for me.

He starts unscrewing the spikes on the right shoe. I start doing the same on the left one. He pulls new spikes out of his pocket. "I needed something from Academy today," he says. "Thought I'd pick up some fresh spikes for your meet tomorrow."

"Thanks," I say.

"Just don't tell your mama."

I glare at Amelia's back. *She's* the one he should be worried about. Anytime Pop tells us, "Don't tell your mama," she's the one who blabs. She can't keep a secret to save her life.

Amelia doesn't seem to be paying attention. She's watching some show about Pokémon. Pop pays for us to have Netflix. He says kids who stay home alone as much as we do shouldn't live in a house with no TV. I wouldn't mind living without a TV, since it's a bunch of noise I don't need, but I realize I'm in the minority. I try not to hold it against the world.

Just because Amelia doesn't seem to be paying attention doesn't mean she isn't.

We're both good at pretending. It's what you learn to do when a dad leaves and a mom tries to fill in all the gaps.

Once Pop's done with my right shoe, he looks at my progress on the left. "You know how to do it?"

"Yeah, I got it."

He never sticks around long on Fridays. Has grown-up things to do on Friday nights, he says. Mom says he has a new girlfriend. He hasn't brought her to meet us yet. The last one tried to convince him square dancing was better for his old bones than running. She didn't last long.

"Okay, then." Pop smacks his bare thighs and stands up. "I've got to get to the golf course."

"I thought you were banned from the golf course again," I say.

"He's always getting banned for one reason or another. The most recent banning happened because he rode his golf cart through a flower bed, blocked the putt of his nemesis, Mr. Allen, with a foot he claimed accidentally got in the way, and threw a rented club in the lake—on purpose—when he swung and missed a ball.

Pop shrugs. "I have friends in high places."

I roll my eyes. "How are you getting there?"

I already know the answer. The golf course is only three miles from here.

"Running," Pop says. He taps on the doorway. "You kids be good." He points at me. "And make sure you get enough sleep. Soak in a salt bath. Eat good food. Remember food is your fuel."

"Okay, Pop."

Before the front door slams, he calls, "And try some baking soda in those shoes!"

Ugh!!!

ROUND 1

I walk into the kitchen. Amelia has her legs propped up on the recliner. She's surfing through the Netflix offerings.

There's not much to choose from that we haven't already seen, but if we have to rewatch an episode of her favorite, *Pony Pals*, I might shrivel up and die.

I peer into the pantry. My stomach is practically eating itself.

And then I see it, pushed way back in the shadows.

The powdered lemonade. Amelia eats it right from the can.

I don't really like the stuff, but that doesn't matter. I shake some into a cup, take the rest of it with me into the living room. I make sure Amelia sees me eat a great big spoonful.

Her mouth drops open.

I eat another spoonful, trying not to let my lips pucker.

"Don't eat all that!" she says.

I shrug. "I saved you some." I pause for just the right amount of time. "It's waiting for you in the kitchen."

She narrows her eyes at me. I sit down on the couch

across from her, lean forward, take another spoonful of lemon powder.

It's grosser than gross, but victory will be worth it.

Amelia slides the footrest down. She scoots forward in the chair. She can see the cup of lemonade powder from where she sits. She looks like she's trying to figure out if she can race into the kitchen and leap back onto the chair before I make myself comfortable.

She doesn't stand a chance.

She tries anyway.

Two steps land me in the chair. I already have the footrest back up, the chair pushed all the way back in the reclining position, before she lands in my lap.

She's easy enough to eject. She weighs about twelve pounds.

She crosses her arms. "Give me back my seat."

I shrug. "It was empty." I hand her the lemonade can. A consolation prize.

She sighs and stomps to the same couch where I sat and watches me, waiting, like it's only a matter of time before I have to get up and she can steal the chair back.

I don't have the heart to tell her I'm not moving until it's time to start supper.

Problem is, I didn't really think about how thirsty that lemonade powder would make me.

Next thing I know, Amelia leaves the living room and walks back in with a glass of ice water. She stares right at me while she slurps it loudly down.

My mouth waters. She grins.

But I will not give her the satisfaction. I'll die of thirst before I surrender the chair.

I lean back and close my eyes. And after a few minutes, I feel Amelia's eyes peel away.

This round goes to me.

Eight

FRIDAY

There's one package of fish sticks left in the freezer. I dig out the last box of macaroni and cheese. I try not to think about the big "payday" Mom starred on the calendar that sits on the old antique table that splits our kitchen and our dining area. The table used to be my mimi's. She was my great-grandmother. She died when I was seven, three years before my nana died.

Still seven more days until payday. What will we eat?

I shove that question away, turn the dial of the oven to four hundred, and line the fish sticks up on a cookie sheet.

"Wrong one," Amelia says.

Mom has two cookie sheets: one she likes to use for our regular fish-sticks-and-french-fries supper, the other she likes to save for cookies, which we hardly ever have.

Even though we wash them, she says she doesn't like the oils to mix. I guess that's something adults understand, because I sure don't.

Amelia takes out the other sheet. They both look exactly the same, down to all their brown spots on the edges.

"How do you know?"

Amelia shrugs. "Just do."

I squint at her back, wondering if she's just trying to get me in trouble. Amelia's sneaky like that. And she holds grudges. She's probably still mad that I had the chair for most of the afternoon.

But I go ahead and use the sheet she took out of the drawer.

My fish sticks make three perfect lines when I slide them in the oven.

Next I start a burner, the flame rising up to meet the bottom of a pot filled with water. The first time I did this, that burner fire scared me, but I've done it so many times now, I hardly worry that a stray spark will set the whole house into flames.

I watch it closely just because . . . well, maybe I do worry a little.

I dump some salt into the water to make it boil faster. I like to have supper ready by the time Mom gets home from work, since it's just one less thing she has to worry about.

I know what it's like carrying a hundred worrisome things in your head. I just want Mom to have a little peace, I guess.

I don't know much about being an adult, but I do know I'm expected to look after Amelia while Mom works, which is every weekday, every Monday, Tuesday, Thursday, and Friday night, most Saturdays, and every Sunday from ten o'clock to four.

Sometimes I feel a little scared being the one in charge when I'm only thirteen, but Amelia knows the rules, so at least there's that. I posted the rules on the refrigerator for easy access, in case anyone forgets.

And by "anyone," I mean Amelia.

House Rules for Staying Home Alone

1. Don't answer the phone. (We still have a landline phone because it's cheaper than a cell phone for Amelia and me. And Mom has to get in touch with us somehow.)
    Amendment one: If you accidentally forget rule number one and answer the phone, don't ever tell someone you're home alone.

Amendment two: If you forget rule number one and amendment number one and accidentally tell the person on the phone that you're home alone, hang up immediately and hide out in your room until you're sure the coast is clear and no one's coming to steal you.

Amendment three: If Mom's the one calling, answer before the answering machine ends the call or she'll FREAK OUT and keep calling.

2. Lock the doors, and do not, under any circumstances, answer the door if someone knocks.

Amendment one: Also do not open the windows.

Amendment two: Do not lift all the blinds. Do not smash your face into the windowpane so you look like a trapped prisoner begging for escape.

3. Stay inside the house at all times while Mom is gone.

4. Do not play with anything dangerous.

Amendment one: "Dangerous" includes but is not limited to matches, toenail clippers, knives, the broom, and Mom's hairbrush.

5. Do not eat everything in the house.
Amendment one: Don't eat half the things in the house.
Amendment two: Don't eat more than two snacks before supper.
Amendment three: Don't eat more than one serving of two snacks before supper.

Amelia's the reason for all the amendments, in case you were wondering. She doesn't do all that well with rules.

Try keeping a kid sister safe when she doesn't do all that well with rules.

Mom looks tired when she gets home. Again. But she smiles when she sees supper laid out on the table.

"Thank you, Leta."

When Mom smiles like that, it makes all my trouble with Amelia completely worth it.

It almost makes me wish for more opportunities like this, when I can help, when I can take some of the burden off Mom, when I can solve problems and let Mom rest.

But lots and lots of days, I just want to be a kid.

Nine

SATURDAY

Mom wakes me up early. She has to drop me off at the school before the sun's even up since I'll ride the bus to the track meet with all my teammates.

She and Pop will drive up later. My race isn't scheduled until the afternoon.

Pop's already sitting at the table, looking damp and sweaty.

"How many miles?" I say.

He grins, holds up seven fingers, and shrugs. *No big deal*, he seems to say without saying.

Mom shakes her head and says, "In the dark. One of these days you'll get run over."

"Not if I'm faster than a car," Pop says.

I laugh. Pop hands me a bag. "I brought some breakfast." It smells like breakfast tacos. My favorite.

But I'll probably give them to Mom. Or pretend I accidentally left them in the car.

Before I'm out the door, Pop says, "Run fast, Leta Lightning Laurel."

That's my favorite nickname. It's something Pop came up with back when I first told him my race was the four hundred. Now I never run at a meet without Pop saying it, just like that, with a little bit of excitement and whole lot of pride.

My chest feels warm and unexplainably tight when I say, "Can't outrun *my* storm."

"Go out there and run like a girl!" Pop practically shouts.

Mom shushes him. "Unless you want to wake up Amelia," she says, eyeing him with one eyebrow raised.

Pop gets quiet real fast. He holds up one thumb.

I hope he can't see my hands shaking when I give him that thumbs-up right back.

I've done this before, I tell myself as Mom weaves through the dark. The dark is *really* dark out here in the middle of nowhere. You can see a billion stars. *This isn't my first track meet.*

But the last track meet didn't come with so much

pressure. I ran for fun. Well, I mean, I ran to win, but it was also fun. Now I *have* to win. I need to prove that I'm the best. I need to practice for the district meet, which is not far enough away. It's my only chance to be remembered. To solve our biggest problems.

Tell me you wouldn't shake under that kind of pressure too.

But I'll be okay. I'm Leta Lightning Laurel.

Before we board the bus, Coach Mac tosses each of us a new uniform. A couple of the girls squeal. "Finally!" someone says.

Our old uniforms are from the 1990s, I think.

"Don't get too excited," Coach Mac says. "They're not new. They're gently used."

"Gently used"? What does that mean?

Coach Mac adds, "We got the boys' hand-me-downs."

"What?" Raina says.

"Uhhh . . . ," Chrissy says.

"There was only enough budget to buy the boys new uniforms," Coach Mac says. "So we get the castoffs." Under her breath, she says, "Just like the last time."

"The last time," meaning the 1990s. So our old uniforms weren't even new back then.

"Why?" I say.

Coach Mac squints at me. "Why do you think, Leta?"

I try my best to come up with a reason, but it's too early. My brain hasn't had time to start firing yet. Plus, I skipped breakfast this morning (I did leave the bag Pop gave me in the car). Coach Mac's monkey bread is practically shouting my name. It won't hurt to have a few pieces of it, right?

Raina raises her hand like we're in class.

Coach Mac lifts her eyebrows at Raina. "Yes, Raina? Do you have a theory?"

"Because the athletics budget goes to the football team, because football is the most important sport at Lolita Junior High," Raina says.

"That's a good theory," Coach Mac says. "Care to add anything to it?"

Raina taps a finger on her cheek. "And whatever money is left goes to boys' sports, not girls'."

Coach Mac points at her like she's just been picked for a prize. "And there's the answer," Coach Mac says.

"Well, that's not fair," I say. "We're not even shaped like boys." I mean, I kind of am still, and so is Chrissy, but Sabrina has boobs, sort of, and Raina's are big enough to complain about, according to her. (Mom's words come back to me: "Big boobs are overrated." Raina says her big boobs make it harder to find sports bras that make running feel comfortable.)

"The world isn't fair," Coach Mac says. "We're women."

"Someone should do something about that," I say. It comes out a little . . . angry. Yeah, I'm angry. What's wrong with being angry? When something's not fair, it should make us all angry.

Coach Mac smirks at me. "You don't think we've been trying for more than a hundred years?" She sighs. "Wearing a castoff boys' uniform isn't giving up, Leta. It's doing what you can when you can do it. I haven't stopped fighting for this track team. For you girls."

She looks tired, just like Mom. Why do so many women look so tired? Is that what growing up does to you? It tires you out? Steals all your energy? Because you have to fight for everything? To be heard, to be taken seriously, to be seen as someone who can do great and remarkable things?

Who wants to grow up, then?

"Now, go try them on," Coach Mac says. "The good news is we have plenty of extras, so if they don't fit, come see me."

We all filter into the locker room. Most of our uniforms fit, although Raina needs a larger top. She rolls her eyes when she puts the exchanged one on. "The rest of it swallows me," she says, flapping the material around her stomach. "Jeez. If there's any wind, I'm gonna turn into a parachute."

We all laugh. Because it's really the only thing you can do, wearing castoff boys' track uniforms.

"I hate living in a patriarchy," Raina says as we walk out the locker room doors together. The bottom of her shirt beats against her stomach. Because of course there's wind.

"You know, in some cultures, the women rule, not the men," Chrissy says.

"I don't want to rule," Raina says. "We don't need to have all the power. Just some. An equal share."

An equal share of power would be nice. And maybe then we'd wear uniforms that actually fit.

How does a person run their best race in a uniform that doesn't fit? I guess we'll find out today.

Coach Mac pulls into the parking lot at Riley Junior High, but before she lets us off the bus, she takes out her clipboard.

Here it comes. The speech she gives us every meet. Some of us could probably recite it for her by now.

"I'm guessing there are several of you on your periods for this meet," she says. She looks up at us. "And some of you who haven't had your first period yet. Which is nothing to worry about. Every body is different, and you're all right on time."

I'm not sure why she tells us this every meet. Maybe to

ease our worries? She says some don't get their first period until high school, and there's nothing wrong with that. I guess when you're in a safe place like this one, where you discuss periods and exchange notes, if you haven't experienced what other people are experiencing, it can make you worry a little. Or make you feel left out, maybe. Coach Mac is just trying to make sure we consider ourselves a team, no matter where we are in our development.

That's my best guess, anyway. My brain's woken up a little now, so I think it's a pretty good guess.

No one giggles uncomfortably or hides their face when Coach Mac starts talking about periods, because this is a safe place. We've made it a safe place. But I wonder, every time we discuss them, are periods safe and comfortable to talk about only when we're in a room of others who have periods? That's kind of sad. How many times in our lives are we *only* in a room of others who have periods?

"Just remember, ladies, your periods do not make you weak," Coach Mac says. "Even if you feel like you're performing worse, you're not. Periods make us powerful."

She tells us this all the time. Coach Mac keeps up with the latest fitness and nutrition research, even though there isn't enough of it about women (she also tells us). But she follows someone who specifically researches female athletes. "Rare," she says. "But long overdue."

Coach Mac taps her pen against her clipboard. "Remember, movement is good for cramps," she says. "And our bodies are miraculous. Once that gun goes off, we do, too, regardless of whether or not we're bleeding." She slides her pen behind her ear. "That said, if anyone needs a heating pad to help with their aches, let me know. Preferably *before* you run. I'd rather not get sweat-soaked heating pads back."

A couple of girls laugh—because it has happened before. And it's very gross.

"Now," Coach Mac says, "let's go get 'em."

"Great pep talk," Chrissy quips to me and Raina. Raina snorts.

"Periods make us powerful," I say, and the three of us crack up again.

Coach Mac eyes us as we step off the bus. "I have extra snacks, too," she says. "For anyone who needs them."

Is she talking to me? Or everyone?

I shake off the question.

"Sports bras?" Coach Mac yells to our backs. "Anybody need a new one?"

The entire team speed-walks away from her.

She's the best coach in the world, but sometimes we have to act like we don't know her.

Ten

SATURDAY

Coach Mac always brings a tent to the meets so we don't get too tired out from the sun and heat. Big orange containers of water and Gatorade sit on a table near one edge of the girls' tent. Blue mats line the ground. Most of the girls stretch out, looking at their phones.

The boys' tent is right beside ours.

When I hear a few boys snickering, I look to see what's so funny. Not that I can see much from here. They're pointing at a piece of paper I can't read, making faces, looking at each other, and laughing behind their hands. Benny is there, along with Quentin, Ryan, and Weston. Benny's the only one not laughing.

The boys' coach, Coach Barnett, tells them to get up

and look alive, their race is starting, so they follow him toward the track.

They leave the paper behind. A corner of it flaps from underneath someone's blanket.

A few girls—Sabrina, Briana, and Brooke—scoot over to the boys' tent. They pick up the paper, make faces, look at each other, and laugh behind their hands, too. "I mean, it's true," Brooke says.

"Totally," Briana says.

"Those girls need to shave," Brooke says.

"And maybe tell their parents to stop being so lazy and get a job," Briana says.

"Or eat less," Brooke says. "Save their parents some money."

I don't know what—or who—they're talking about, but my whole body turns into a fire.

Briana and Brooke bring the paper to the girls' tent, and when they head toward the concession stand and leave it right there in the open, I consider it my invitation to pick it up.

And then wish I hadn't.

It's a series of lists. *Girls with the Straightest Teeth. Girls with the Longest Hair. Girls with the Best Bodies.* Seven lists in all.

I make three of their lists:

Girls with the Hairiest Legs

Girls with the Smelliest Shoes

Girls from the Poorest Families

My face burns like I've spent all day in the sun instead of under this tent.

Benny saw the lists. And he didn't say a word.

Sometimes boys are the worst.

Sabrina, Briana, and Brooke return from the concession stand. Briana eyes the paper still in my hand. She glances at Brooke, and both of them look like they're trying hard not to laugh.

When I meet Sabrina's eyes, she shrugs.

Sabrina saw the list too. And she didn't say a word either.

Sometimes girls are the worst.

I don't have time for this nonsense.

I grab my smelly, flapping-sole shoes and stalk away from the tent.

I have a race to run.

I have a race to win.

The Run: Part 1

The worst part is standing there, waiting for your heat to be called, maybe doing some high knees or butt kicks so the nervous energy has someplace to go and you can pretend you're not sizing up the competition, trying to see how you compare.

No, the worst part is the moment after they call your heat and you move to your lane while sizing up the competition, trying to see how you compare.

No, the worst part is getting into the starting blocks, heart already pounding so hard you're afraid you're losing valuable energy, hoping you remember how to do this.

No, the worst part is when the woman calls out, "On your mark," and every muscle in your legs tenses.

No, the worst part is when she calls out, "Get set," and your legs push your butt into the air so they can blast you from the blocks and your heart feels like it might gallop right out of your chest and you'd be left there gasping because you have nothing left to power you through the lap.

No, the worst part is that tiny little split of a second before the gun goes off and your body launches into action.

No, the worst part is when someone has a false start and you have to do it all over again, hoping you're not the false start this time.

No, the worst part is when your mind wanders to the stands and you see the empty seat beside your mom that you always see but have never quite managed to ignore.

No, the worst part is when the gun goes off the second time and you execute the perfect launch and find your rhythm in the first three steps but realize the word in your mind that lines up with your foot strikes sounds a lot like

Forgettable

Forgettable

Forgettable.

The Run: Part 2

The best part is when you fly past the first curve and the rhythm changes, long strides replacing short steps.

No, the best part is when you wrestle that ugly word, "forgettable," to the ground, trample it under your brand-new sharp spikes, and let your mind find better ones you remember your pop telling you ages ago: *Run the race you're in.*

No, the best part is pulling ahead on that straightaway, now in front, everyone else behind.

No, the best part is sprinting the next curve, wind blazing against you, knowing it doesn't matter, you have more to give. Enough to give.

No, the best part is flying toward the finish, feeling that left sole flap, hearing the words change into a cry of victory: *I will win in my smelly, flappy shoes! Take that!*

No, the best part is doing it all again for the finals heat.

No, the best part is feeling that smile split your face just before you cross the finish line first.

No, the best part is hearing Pop shout from the stands, "And that's how it's done, folks," and not even wishing he'd sit back down and shut his mouth.

No, the best part is hearing the other coaches congratulate Coach Mac, listening to the runners say, "Great race," knowing you're anything but forgettable today. They will remember your name.

The whole world will remember you.

But more important, *he* will remember you.

Eleven

SATURDAY

Coach Mac pulls me up. "Don't bend over like that," she says. "Lungs can't get air when they're folded in half."

She sends me off the track, walking backward. I still have the mile relay in another hour.

The third four hundred of the day.

But I've trained for this.

Coach Mac walks me back to the tent. And even though I expect her to gush over me, or at least congratulate me for my great run, all she says is, "If I ever see you cross the finish line like a beauty queen again, I will make you run so many four hundreds, you will lose all feeling in your feet."

What?!

Coach Mac stops, puts one hand on her hip, and uses

the other to gesture in the general direction of her face. "You were smiling so wide I thought your face might split open. You hadn't even won the race yet!"

Oh.

But I *knew* I was going to win by that point. Doesn't that count?

Not for Coach Mac.

"I'm not against runners smiling," Coach Mac says, which is confusing, because it sounds like she is. She clarifies, "But you run your hardest, and you shouldn't have the energy to smile like that." She parodies me, pulling her lips into a grotesquely wide smile with her fingers. I wrinkle my nose. I think she's being dramatic. There's no way I looked like that. "That tells me you have more to give."

Isn't she happy I broke my personal record? I ran my hardest!

But then Coach Mac says, "You'll need more to give to win district."

I'm not sure I know how to give more. I ran a personal best!

Coach Mac turns away like she's said all that needs saying. Then she turns back around.

I wait for her belated congratulations, her "Great job, Leta," her "I always knew you could run like a pro."

But all she says is "And we need to have a talk about those shoes."

I hear Briana and Brooke giggle. I don't bother to check if Sabrina's with them.

We won the mile relay, too, no thanks to Sabrina.

She had the worst split out of the four of us. She blamed it on Raina's handoff, but Raina says she handed off perfectly, just like we all practiced. And I believe her.

Both of us are in sour moods on the bus ride home. Mom took Pop and Amelia home right after the relay. She said Amelia had been complaining about the "terrible, melting heat" since right after lunch.

I don't mind. The bus is usually fun. At least when you get to ride with your three best friends, who are also on your winning mile relay team.

Sabrina sat with Briana and Brooke, though. Every time I look at her way up there in the front of the bus, she seems like she's having a grand time.

Are they giggling about the lists?

My face feels like it did that day I stood too close to the fire Mom burns when she needs to get rid of trash. The houses out where we live don't have trash pickup like they do in the city. We have to figure out what to do with it ourselves.

"Don't worry about them," Chrissy says, glancing at Sabrina and the other girls. Maybe that's easy for her to say. She hasn't known Sabrina since she was in kindergarten. Sabrina's the only friend who's ever been to my house.

It's too complicated to tell you why. But it has something to do with how embarrassed I feel about the peeling paint and the sagging floors and the shabby furniture. I know Chrissy lives in a trailer, but it's in better shape than my house. And Raina's grandma's house is one of those fancy brick ones. Sabrina lives in a two-story house that could fit three of my houses in it. But I never worried about it before.

She never acted like this before.

Sabrina knows a lot of my secrets. And I'm not sure if I can trust her to keep them anymore.

Coach Mac catches me on my way off the bus. I expect her to say something about my shoes since she said we needed to talk about them, so it surprises me when she says, "Come Monday, a new girl's joining the team."

Natalie Dash. My stomach gets tight.

Coach Mac's voice is quiet, like she's telling me secrets. I understand why when she says, "She raced at her old school." Pause. "Her race was the four hundred."

So it's true. I was hoping the rumors were like most rumors at Lolita Junior High and also anything Pop says his friend Marty watches on some cable news channel: wildly exaggerated and laughably false. My heart starts beating like I'm lined up at the starting blocks.

"We can have two runners who race the four hundred," Coach Mac says. "That's not a problem." Pause. "But I want you to know she's real good."

What is she trying to tell me—that Natalie is faster than me?

Coach Mac pats me on the shoulder. "I think we haven't seen all Leta Laurel can do, though."

She is. She's saying Natalie Dash is faster than me. What's her best time? How many races has she won? How does a person give more when she already feels like she's giving everything?

Mom would say that's the question of a woman's world. But I'm not thinking about a woman's world right now. I'm thinking about mine.

And all those questions get caught in my throat. I stare at the sky, sliding toward sunset with a rainbow of colors. It's much happier than I am.

My insides knot and churn. I feel like I've just eaten too

much of Chrissy's mom's homemade enchiladas, which are heavy on the cheese. And so greasy you can practically see your reflection in them.

"You ran well today, Leta," Coach Mac says. I can't even claim the victorious feeling that would normally come with her admission, finally, because I feel so sick. She leans closer to me. "But I know you've got more in you." She taps a fist to her heart on the last words. "I'm just waiting for you to show me you can run your race."

The words don't make the least bit of sense, since I *have* shown Coach Mac I can run my race. But she doesn't bother clarifying. She moves toward her car, lifts a hand, and says, "Rest those legs tomorrow. See you Monday."

Mom's waiting in the parking lot. I'm glad she's not late. I don't need another thing to worry about right now.

"Wow, did you run today," she says when I slide into the car. I see her glance down at my feet, then look away real quick.

Did she see my sole flapping when I ran? Did everybody see? Will it be all over the school by Monday?

"I am just so amazed," Mom says. "I don't know how you or your pop do it."

Her words feel like one of those sparkling waters Pop

stocks in our fridge every now and then: fizzy, refreshing, so filling they might burst seams.

"Pop ordered pizza," Mom says after a while. "Says you deserve it after all that hard running."

Pizza sounds divine. Maybe I'll blot the top with a paper towel, like all those magazines tell me I should do. So the calories are blotted away.

Maybe I *can* give more—the more Coach Mac wants to see—by getting lighter on my feet. Lighter is faster. I know Coach Mac said that's a myth, but it makes total sense. How could you not be faster if you were lighter?

And Briana was right. Eating less *would* save Mom money. I'd accomplish two things at the same time.

I nod to myself. No one even has to know.

The road hums under our tires for a long time before I finally get the courage to say, "Mom?"

"Yeah, baby?"

"How often are you supposed to shave your legs?" I try not to rub a hand over mine, but they suddenly itch, and I scratch. It's been a while since I shaved them. Maybe a week or two?

Mom glances at me, then back at the road. "There's not a rule," she says. "It depends on the person."

"How do you know when it's time to shave again?"

Mom bites her lip. I know she's probably thinking about how she never got to teach me how to shave, because one day I came home from fifth grade after a boy, Collin Blake, made fun of my "hairy gorilla legs" and took Mom's razor and shaved every strand of dark brown away. My legs felt so soft and silky, but Mom's reaction was not soft and silky. It was very loud and very prickly.

Apparently a daughter shaving her legs for the first time is a big deal or something. Mom said I'd probably regret it, because once you shaved, you'd always feel like you had to keep shaving. She was right about that. And she'd wanted me to have a choice, she'd said. "Your body, your choice. For everything," she'd said.

But how do you *really* have a choice, when people point out your hairy legs in fifth grade?

I don't like shaving, to be honest. First of all, I have long legs and it takes forever to do it. Second of all, as soon as you're done, the hair starts growing back. Third of all, no matter what kind of razor we try—sensitive; super sensitive; super, super sensitive—I still end up with irritated red bumps everywhere. And fourth of all, who said I couldn't have hair on my legs in the first place?

Sometimes I let weeks go by between my shaves. It never bothered me before now.

"I guess you shave again when the hair gets itchy," Mom says. "Or you feel uncomfortable. Or . . ." She seems flustered, like she can't really think of a good answer.

Mom's thoughts seem to have traveled in the same direction as mine, because she says, "It's kind of stupid, really. Your leg hair wouldn't get itchy if you didn't shave it in the first place. And shaving when you feel uncomfortable . . . that's letting someone else's opinion have power over you." She shakes her head. "What a ridiculous standard."

"But not so unusual in a woman's world, right?" I say.

Mom smiles sadly at me. She doesn't have to answer.

"I don't have to shave if I don't want to," I say. It's just something to say. Junior high is brutal enough without "hairy gorilla legs." Thanks, Collin Blake, for the negative voice you contributed to my head back in fifth grade. He doesn't even go to our school anymore. It shouldn't matter.

Why does it matter?

Because I made a list today. For not shaving my legs in a week or two.

Mom squeezes my hairy knee. "You don't have to shave if you don't want to," she agrees, then adds, "You don't have to do anything you don't want to do."

Mom's words make me feel free—the way I should feel all the time.

But then I think of that list, and the cage closes right back around me.

"The world is a vampire," Mom told me once. It was a quote from one of her brother's favorite songs.

I didn't realize then that it was true. That the world would work so hard to suck away my confidence and my courage and my value and my belief that I was made for something great.

Is this what it means to be a young woman?

How do you win against a vampire?

Twelve

SATURDAY

Pop and Amelia have already eaten half a pizza by the time Mom and I get home. But two more wait on the counter, so I don't mind much.

I watch Mom closely. She takes only one piece of pizza. But she doesn't blot the top with a napkin like I do. That gives me room for at least another slice.

I put two on my plate, blot, and then eat them slowly.

Pop goes on and on and on about the meet. I halfway listen until he says, "When's district?"

"Two weeks."

Two weeks to practice running that track lap, accounting for every possibility (including a new potentially fast girl), making sure I bring home the district title so the newspapers go wild, so Mom clips the article about my win and mails it to Dad, so he remembers he has a daughter named Leta Laurel and she's a (kind of) famous runner and maybe he should check in with her, at least send some money for food and probably new track shoes so she can keep winning races.

"Leta?" Pop says. "You hear me, or are you stuck in your own victorious world, imagining the winner's gold?"

I wouldn't call it a victorious world. But I shrug and offer Pop a half smile.

"I said, do you need anything before the big race?" He clears his throat and glances at Mom.

Mom looks at me, waiting. I don't want to ask for anything. We can't afford anything.

I think of my shoes. Pop's probably thinking about my shoes too. But he already got me some new spikes. It's not like he has a lot of money either. I can't ask him to do more. Especially not in front of Mom. She's sensitive about taking money from Pop. I don't completely understand it, but it has something to do with feeling like she's failing because she needs a little extra support.

Even though, if Dad were here, she'd have more support.

That's the world for you, though. Making my mom, who already works two jobs, feel like a failure. Making Dad feel like a winner because he somehow gets out of paying to feed and clothe his kids. If that doesn't convince you the world's not fair, I don't know what will.

I'll figure out what to do with my old shoes. I'll put another layer of superglue on them. Maybe an inch of superglue will make them springier. Like the foam bottoms of those fancy, expensive shoes.

I shake my head. "I have my legs and my feet and my arms that keep swinging." He tells me this any time I ask him if he needs anything for his big races—which are way bigger than mine, if you're looking at mileage.

Pop grins at me. "Using my own words against me, I see."

"What else are they good for?"

Pop laughs the kind of bubbling laugh that makes you feel like you're fully alive and headed toward triumph. I want to hug him for that.

Before Pop leaves, he says, "I'm real proud of you, Leta. You ran your race today."

The words sound a little weird but also true.

In my head, I say, *See, Coach Mac? Pop, who's practically a professional runner, thinks I ran my race. Why don't you?*

He kisses the top of my head.

"You need a ride home, Dad?" Mom says.

Pop waves a hand. "I'm running."

He lives a whole six miles from us, in town. And it's dark. I know he ran in the dark this morning, but nighttime seems worse.

"You can't run home this late," I say, glancing at Mom.

Pop switches on a light he straps across his forehead and presses a button on his belt that makes him blink all over like a Christmas tree.

"Watch me," he says, and he leaps off our porch and takes off running. Before he gets to the end of the driveway, he calls, "See y'all tomorrow."

"That man," Mom says, the words half laughter.

I fill in the blank.

That man is nuts.

That man is brave.

That man is one great grandpa.

I wait until Mom's in bed before I ask Amelia, "Dad call today?"

"No."

I didn't expect him to, but I still say, "You sure? You checked the machine?"

"Mom did."

I didn't expect him to, but I still think, *Maybe Mom doesn't want to tell us.*

"There weren't any messages on the machine," Amelia says. "The light wasn't blinking."

I didn't expect him to, but I still feel the way her words turn my legs to stone.

Like no matter how hard I run, I will never be able to run away from being "forgettable," which is really just another way of saying "never good enough."

Thirteen

SUNDAY

Of course I run on Sunday, even though I'm not supposed to.

I'm out bright and early, Coach Mac's words chasing me.

I know you've got more in you.

I try to find it.

But four hundred after four hundred after four hundred, I fail.

I hope something's wrong with my watch and not my feet.

Sixteen four hundreds in, I see a bike turn out of Benny Dunlap's driveway.

My heart feels like I just sprinted a whole mile, but I keep going, legs deadening, feet not wanting to pick themselves up right.

And when I see who's on the bike, I wish I'd already quit or at least run a four hundred in the other direction.

I don't know who else I expected, but of course it's Benny.

It's four hundred meters from my house to the edge of his family's property. They keep cows there. It's another four hundred meters in that same direction to his long gravel driveway.

I haven't crossed his property line this whole time, but something tells me I wasn't invisible, either. The land's so flat you can see clear across for miles.

I turn around and pretend I'm heading back to my house. I don't have four hundred meters measured from my driveway to the next neighbor's property on the other side, but maybe I'll guess it.

"Hey." Benny hops off his bike, pushes it along beside me. "Why're you out here?"

It's the same thing I want to ask him.

I shrug. "Practicing."

"Aren't you supposed to take a day off after a meet? That's what Coach Barnett makes us do."

I shrug again. Maybe you can take time off if you don't want to win as badly as I do. Of course I don't say that out loud. Instead, I say, "I like running."

And I think I mostly mean it.

"That was an awesome race yesterday," Benny says. "You beat everybody by at least twenty meters."

I don't think it was that much. I try to smile, but inside I'm thinking, *It wasn't good enough, though. It needs to be better.*

If I want my picture in the newspaper, if I want Mom to send that clipping to Dad, if I want him to remember he's got a daughter named Leta and another daughter named Amelia, I'll have to do better than twenty meters and a personal record. I'll have to break all the records.

We've reached my driveway. I want to do another four hundred—maybe another sixteen of them—but I don't want to do them with Benny watching.

I don't want to be put on another list. Like Runners with the Worst Worn-Out Shoes or Girls Who Sweat Profusely or Ugliest Female Racers.

"Listen, Leta," Benny starts to say, but then the words sort of stop.

"I need to run a few more," I say after a second. Benny doesn't take the hint.

He says, "Care for some competition?"

Benny runs the two-hundred-meter dash, but he's pretty good at the four hundred. His first two he starts out way too fast—like it's more sprint than endurance. But then he seems to realize it's both.

He keeps pace with me, even after eight of them. So I push harder. I pull ahead. I take everything I have and pour it into my legs.

The first time I beat him is four hundred number ten, which is really my twenty-sixth.

And at the exact moment when I tease Benny about getting beat by a girl, a voice behind me yells, "Atta girl, Leta! How's it feel to lose a race to a girl, young man?"

I turn in slow motion, already knowing what I'll find.

Pop, in the brightest yellow shorts I've ever seen. I need some sunglasses. They hurt my eyes.

I wish that was the worst part, but it's not. The shorts are barely longer than the suits those male swimmers wear in the Olympics. And he's wearing a running backpack, but under that? He's shirtless.

If the ground opened up and swallowed me now, I would not even put up a fight.

Benny smiles at Pop. "Doesn't feel any different than getting beat by a boy."

Pop grins and points a finger. "Now, that's a smart boy," he says to me. "And that's the right answer," he says to Benny.

He turns down our driveway, water sloshing in his backpack. The water is hidden in a "bladder," which sounds a little gross, I know, but it holds enough water for his long runs. The bladder has a tube stretching from it that clips to his vest so he can take easy sips without using his hands or breaking his stride. It's a useful thing to have because hydration is important when you're a runner. Pop says you can lose whole minutes off miles if you're not properly hydrated.

"How many miles, Pop?" I yell to his back.

"I took it easy today," Pop says, avoiding my question. He probably doesn't want to make me look bad in front of Benny.

But I think maybe I've put in more miles than he has today, so I say, "I've got almost seven."

Pop turns at the sagging porch. "That's a good start." I smile until he adds, "Only seventeen more to catch me."

I shake my head, then remember who's here with me.

What kind of list will Benny put me on now? Girls with the Weirdest Grandpas?

But he's staring toward Pop open-mouthed. After a second he says, "Wow. How's a person run so many miles when they're that old?"

I can't help but laugh.

Fourteen

SUNDAY

I do six more four hundreds once Benny leaves. My pace slows with every one. It's probably time to quit.

Pop stands at the dining room window, which faces the road. I know he's probably been watching me this whole time.

He waits until I've poured myself a big, tall glass of ice water before he says, "Why are you out there the day after your track meet?"

I tell him the same thing I told Benny. "Practicing."

"Don't you get enough of that with your coach?"

I shrug. "I just felt like running."

Pop turns from the window. "You like running, Leta?"

Of course I like running. What kind of ridiculous question is that? Would I do it if I didn't like it? Would anyone?

"Yeah," I say. "I may even love it."

Pop nods. "Why do you like running so much?"

I guess I've never thought about it. So I say, "I don't really know."

Pop stares back out the window. "Me, I like running because it's a time I can be with myself. I can think about the things I love in my life. The people. I can forgive people who need forgiving, accept the things I can't change, and find peace with what I've done or haven't done."

He sounds like a philosopher. The words settle between us like a minute-long rest after a two-hundred-meter sprint instead of the typical thirty-second one.

Unexpected. Needed. Welcome.

Pop turns round to look at me again. "Do you like running so much because you're running away from something or toward something else?"

I guess I've never really thought about this, either. "Maybe both?" I say. Is that wrong?

Pop nods. "Long as you're not just running away." Then, so quiet it's hard to hear: "There's not a thing in this world that can be solved by running away."

Mom's still at work when Pop leaves. Amelia and I both wave him out the door.

He doesn't run this time. He walks, staring up at the sky.

"You think Pop's okay?" Amelia says. Even she noticed his quiet, like he was somewhere else all morning.

I don't really know what's gotten into Pop or if he'll be okay, but a big sister should never tell her little sister that. So I say, "Of course he'll be okay. He's superhuman."

Amelia cracks up. But it doesn't take her long to stop laughing. "There's not anything to eat in the pantry."

"Sure there is." But when I look, it's almost completely bare. I pull out a can of green beans. "Want to share?"

Amelia wrinkles her nose. "Not really."

But when we open the fridge, it's empty, too, except for a jar of mayonnaise and one old carrot so flimsy it might be made of rubber.

"Looks like green beans for today's snack," I say.

Amelia sighs.

"I'm sure Mom will stop by the store on her way home," I say.

I'm not sure. Payday is still five days away. But no sense in worrying Amelia with the question that won't leave me in peace:

What if she doesn't?

Round 2

Amelia opens the bathroom door and eyes the chair that's now empty since I thought I had more time to pour myself another glass of ice water.

She meets my eyes before glancing back at the chair, like she's trying to decide if she should have mercy or be her usual thieving self. I know exactly what she's thinking. Every muscle in my body tenses, waiting.

The world stills for a second, all activity suspended, before Amelia lunges in the direction of the chair, and I lunge to meet her, my battle cry so loud and fierce it feels like it shakes the walls.

I collide with her, and my force sends us both skidding toward the wall, socks sliding on linoleum. Amelia hits first before I slam into her.

It surprises me how quickly she shoves me away and makes another lunge for the chair, one arm gripping the armrest, dragging her toward it while I drag her away. She's stronger than she looks. Our feet slip and slide like we're in Rollerblades. I knock Amelia's feet out from under her, but she grips the armrest like it's a log keeping her from drowning. I growl, one arm around her waist, the hand of the other peeling her fingers off one by one.

She kicks my feet and knocks me down, but she's lost her grip on the chair, so she rolls down with me. I body-slam her toward the doorway and away from the chair, but just as I'm about to claim victory, her head jams into my side. I scramble for balance, my feet groping at the slippery floor, and then I see my chance. I give Amelia a mighty shove. She flies into the couch and I fall into the chair, raise the leg rest, and spread out as much as I can.

I know what's coming.

Amelia launches herself into my lap, but I'm ready. I use every muscle to launch her back out.

"Haha!" I shout, heart pounding, breath heaving.

Amelia growls in frustration until she sees the glass of ice water I poured myself. Then she throws me a wicked smile, stalks to the counter, and gulps it down herself.

Well, most of it. She uses the last gulp to spit back into the glass so an inch of backwash remains.

"Thanks for the water," she says.

Sometimes it's hard to tell who wins.

Fifteen

SUNDAY

It's almost four before I realize no one checked the mail yesterday. We were all at my track meet, and if Mom had checked the mail, it would be piled on the cracked wooden dresser she calls a buffet—which has never and likely will never have a buffet of food spread on it, however hard my stomach wishes it would.

There's no pile of mail.

So I surrender the chair to Amelia, who flies into it so fast she nearly tips it over. "Haha!" she screams, like I didn't give it up on purpose.

By the time she realizes why I surrendered it, I'm too far ahead for her to catch.

Amelia loves to check the mail.

I grab the load in one fist and race back to the house. "You're not supposed to be outside while Mom's not here!" I yell behind me.

Amelia lets loose a roar that sounds almost more animal than human. I lose a few seconds laughing, since laughing makes it hard to breathe. But I still beat her by at least a minute. By the time she slams through the front door, I'm already in the chair, sorting through the pile.

"I hate you," Amelia says.

She doesn't mean that. At least, I don't think she does.

I toss her half the mail, a consolation prize.

Amelia gets distracted by a magazine with all sorts of clothes you can buy through the mail. I don't know why they send these things to Mom. It's been years since she bought herself anything.

Nothing good was in my pile, so I say, "Hand me the rest of that."

Amelia gives me the kind of look that could make a tree dry up and die. She closes the magazine and flips through the envelopes.

Most of them are probably bills. I try not to notice their bright yellow PAST DUE tags. Last year we didn't have heat for the first four weeks of winter because Mom couldn't afford to get our propane tank filled up. Which meant we also had to eat microwaved meals since our stove runs on gas. When Pop got back from the trip he takes to see Mom's brother in Florida every year, he called the gas company immediately and paid to have the tank filled. We had heat the next day and could fold up all the extra blankets.

"This one's different," Amelia says, tearing me from thoughts that would likely send me spiraling if she weren't here. Money makes me feel anxious. Instability makes me feel anxious. Not knowing if we'll be able to afford something we need makes me feel anxious. I don't ever tell Mom these things.

Amelia holds up an envelope. Instead of a typed *Ms. Laurel* and address like all the others, it says *Shirley Laurel* and is handwritten, not typed.

"Let me see it?" I say.

I expect Amelia to say, "Come and get it," but she just tosses it to me.

The handwriting looks familiar, all caps instead of caps with lowercase. My heart feels like I've just run twelve four hundreds.

Dad?

Did he finally remember us?

I glance at Amelia and tear open the envelope.

"Isn't that for Mom?" Amelia says.

"Doesn't matter," I say.

But it does matter. I see that as soon as I open it.

It's not a letter from Dad. It's a letter from his mom, my granny.

A picture falls out of the envelope. Dad and . . . someone else. A woman. With raven-black hair and icy blue eyes. She is not Mom. Clearly. But Dad has his arm around her like they're . . . I don't know, boyfriend and girlfriend or something.

My throat goes dry. I flip over the picture. *Brian and his new girlfriend*, someone's written. Judging by the handwriting, it was probably Granny. She wrote a date under the words too. Less than two months ago.

A heavy feeling starts sweeping down my body. It settles in my chest and stomach.

"What is it?" Amelia says.

"Nothing." I try to stuff the picture back in the letter before Amelia can see it. I try not to read the letter, but words swim in my eyes. *Girlfriend . . . lives with her . . . been going on for the last five years.*

I don't know what it all means, but I also do.

"What is it?" Amelia says again.

"Nothing." My voice is probably a little too harsh. I shove the envelope back into the pile. I'll have to explain to

Mom why it's open, tell her I didn't read it, pretend I didn't see that picture.

Amelia hurls herself right into my lap, wrestles the envelope from me. Before I can do anything, the picture falls out again. She looks at it, her head cocked to the side.

"Who's this with Dad?" she says.

And since there's no way around it, I say, "Dad's girlfriend."

She looks at me with eyes so wide they could swallow the world.

I sure wish they would.

Here's what I don't understand . . . but do, sort of.

Mom and Dad are still married.

How does Dad have a girlfriend? Isn't that wrong? Like, isn't he supposed to be *here*, with us, instead of *there*, with her? We were here first.

And what if . . .

What if he has more kids, with her, and he decides they're the ones who are unforgettable, not me and Amelia? What if he leaves us for good? What if Amelia never gets a daddy-daughter dance with her actual dad?

"Never" is a really hard word to swallow.

Sixteen

SUNDAY

I'm out running again when Mom pulls into the driveway.

"Leta? What are you doing out here?"

"Practicing," I yell, and set myself up for another four hundred.

My shins are on fire, my feet feel like they picked up a few nails, and my arms are so numb I probably look like a toddler trying to run for the first time.

"I think you've done enough practicing, sweetie," Mom says.

How does she know?

But it's not enough. It will never be enough. I have to win district champion. I have to get faster.

"Just a few more," I say.

"Leta."

I know that voice. Mom uses it when she wants no arguing. When she has shut down the conversation and there's no room for negotiation. She doesn't use it often. She only uses it when it matters.

I sigh and head toward her. She stands waiting, hands on her hips. When I'm just a few steps from her, she says, "You know you can injure yourself if you don't let your body rest."

Did Pop tell her that? Because Mom's not a runner.

But I know she's right. I just don't have time for rest.

Mom puts her arm around me and gives me a quick squeeze. "Help me unload groceries."

My mood lifts a little knowing she got groceries, knowing our pantry won't be empty for long. Knowing we'll have something special tonight, which is a grocery-trip reward. Mom always picks up something different, like pizza or lasagna.

When I see the groceries in the back, my mood plummets again.

She could have unloaded those two bags herself.

I guess Mom sees something on my face, because she says, "I'll get more when payday rolls around."

Payday, still five days away.

I nod, blink hard, and try not to think about all those past-due bills. Why doesn't she just ask for help? Why doesn't she call Dad and demand he send money? We're still his daughters. She's still his wife. I know she shouldn't have to ask for money. He should be sending it regularly, or he should be made to send it regularly. But has she tried telling him what's going on here? Would he even care?

There has to be something I can do.

I glance toward the street. I won't run any more tonight. But I will give my all every day until district.

I never get a chance to tell Mom why that letter was open, so when she knocks on my bedroom door and says, "Can I talk to you a minute, Leta?" I think I know what it's about.

I glance at Amelia, who's stretched out on her trundle bed, but she pretends to be engrossed in the book she's opened. It looks like it might be another Goosebumps one. I don't know why she reads them. They scare her into needing a night-light. And it's hard for me to sleep with a night-light. That's one of the worst things about sharing a room—you have to compromise on everything.

I don't like compromising.

I step over Amelia on my way out and follow Mom to her bedroom.

Her bed fills practically the entire room, with only a

small space on either side for two tiny tables. A lamp's yellow glow makes the comforter look more green than blue.

Mom holds up the opened letter. I look at the rust-colored carpet, afraid of what I'll see if I meet her eyes.

"I found this with all the mail," she says.

I nod. Yeah. Me too.

Mom sighs.

"I'm sorry I opened it," I tell the floor. "I thought it might be a letter from Dad." Only now do I realize that also wouldn't have given me a reason to open it. It was addressed to Mom.

The quiet in the room feels so heavy it's hard to breathe. I squeeze words into it. "Did you know?"

This time I look at Mom. Her eyes hold so much pain, I wish I hadn't asked. "I had my suspicions," she says. Her eyes drop to the letter, and she takes out the picture. "I don't think I wanted to believe it, so I just . . ." She lets whatever she was going to say trail off. I have no idea how to fill in the blank. She just ignored it? Pretended everything was normal? Believed things would work out?

I swallow hard. "He lied."

I didn't mean to say the words out loud, but my mouth has a mind of its own. Mom takes my hand.

"I know, baby."

"He said he'd see us soon. He said he was coming back."

Mom doesn't say anything, but her hand squeezes mine harder.

"But he forgot about us instead."

"Oh, Leta." Mom pulls me into her arms and kisses the top of my head. My eyes blur and spill. She holds me for a long time.

But what she doesn't do is tell me Dad didn't forget about me and Amelia.

Amelia's already stretched out in her bed, light off, when I leave Mom's room. At first I think I've missed our good night ritual, but just as I pull the covers up to my chin, she says, "Good night, Leta."

"Good night, Amelia."

"Sweet dreams."

"Sweet dreams."

"See you in the morning."

"Okay. See you in the morning."

"Okay. Love you."

"Love you, too."

I wait for her breathing to even out, but after several minutes it's still as erratic as she is most days. And then she says, "Dad's not coming back, is he?"

My throat hurts when I say, "I don't know, Amelia."

She doesn't say anything else, just turns to face the door.

Tomorrow I'll start training even harder. I have to win that race. I have to.

All night I dream about a new girl so fast I can't catch her.

Seventeen

MONDAY

My English teacher, Mrs. Crisp, starts class the next day with "I have a new project for you all!"

Usually, I love our English projects. But when she tells us this is a letter project loosely based off the book we just finished reading, *Dear Mr. Henshaw* by Beverly Cleary, I sag. I sag even more when she says, "I want you all to pick five people you'll write some letters to. You can write to parents or grandparents or someone from history or friends or someone younger than you or siblings. Five people who are important to you. But here's the catch." Mrs. Crisp holds up her finger. "I want you to make sure you include someone you love, someone you admire, someone you'd like to know better, someone who hurt you, and someone who meant a lot to you but isn't around anymore." She looks at each of us as she explains.

I wonder how many of my classmates can think of one person who meets all five of those things. I can.

"You'll write four of these people one letter each," Mrs. Crisp continues. "And you'll write the last person four letters. So that's eight total letters."

Someone groans. It's exactly the way I feel. Mrs. Crisp just smiles.

"You'll use these letters to bare your soul," she says. "And no one will know except me. Unless you choose to share."

Baring our souls sounds way too hard. And so does picking five people I'd like to write letters to.

I sit there staring at my blank piece of paper for a long, long time.

The one person I want to write to wouldn't care, would he?

We don't even have his address. I looked in Mom's book last night. No address, no phone number, nothing to tell me he even exists anymore.

I sigh.

"Leta?" Mrs. Crisp's voice is almost a whisper. She squats beside me, her eyes flicking from my page, which is still completely blank, to my face. *You don't usually have trouble with my assignments*, her eyes seem to say.

And it's true. English is usually one of my favorite subjects, right behind science.

A lump curls up in the back of my throat.

"Having trouble getting started?" Mrs. Crisp says.

"I don't know who to write to," I whisper.

Mrs. Crisp nods. "You could start with a list," she says. "People in your life who fit into each category." She drops her voice. "I'm not telling everyone this, but if you can't think of anyone in one particular category, you could write to someone imaginary. But only one."

Someone imaginary. Maybe that's all Dad ever really was.

"And you can write letters to yourself. A younger self or an older self. That could be the 'someone you love.'"

Do I love myself? I've never really thought about it.

Mrs. Crisp moves away before I can thank her for all her ideas, but I still feel eyes on me. I look around the room and see the new girl, Natalie, staring right at me, like she can see into the deepest, darkest places I have.

It's a very uncomfortable feeling.

She holds my gaze for a whole minute before dropping her eyes back to her paper, which looks like it's filled with words.

I bite the end of my pen, take a deep breath, and write,

Dear Dad.

But when no words come after that, I scratch it out. I try another. *Dear Leta.*

Scratch that one out too.

By the time the bell rings, I'm no closer to a letter than I was when class started.

I guess some letters aren't all that easy to write.

Eighteen

MONDAY

Raina and Chrissy jog the warm-up lap with me before heading off to help each other stretch. Sabrina and I usually stretch together, since we both have long legs. But she's already teamed up with Ginger Banks. Raina and Chrissy have shorter legs and are the perfect partners. I can't ask them to break up their partnership just because Sabrina's being weird.

"Why aren't you stretching, Leta?" Coach Mac calls out. Sabrina looks my way but doesn't meet my eyes.

I shrug. "No partner."

Then I see the new girl, standing alone.

Coach Mac sees her too. "Natalie," she says. "Stretch with Leta."

Natalie heads in my direction. A couple of the girls give

her a dirty look, including Raina and Chrissy. When Natalie passes her, Brooke wrinkles her nose and rolls her eyes at Natalie's back, like Natalie smells or something.

I haven't heard Natalie say a word since track practice started, and she stays quiet all through the stretching, too.

That's fine by me. I don't feel like talking anyway.

Especially to a new girl who might be faster than me.

Coach Mac blows her whistle, and we all move to the starting line for four-hundred-meter repeats, today's workout. We never know how many we'll do. Coach Mac likes to say it depends on how we run them—if we run hard, we'll run fewer. But we always do at least six.

My legs feel tired from yesterday. So I make sure to fall back with Raina and Chrissy and avoid Natalie.

But halfway to six, Coach Mac calls out, "Get those feet moving, Leta. You're slow as a sloth today." Which is totally not true. I'm *way* faster than a sloth—have you seen how they move? But I know what she's saying. She's saying Natalie's clocking faster splits than I am.

I try to pick it up, but my shins feel like they're passing through a field of brambles.

"What's wrong with you today, Leta?" Coach Mac glares at my shoes. Is this a question I'll be getting forever now? Didn't she ask this last practice?

No. It's moved from "What's wrong with your feet?" to "What's wrong with you?" It feels sharp and painful to swallow. If people knew what their careless words did to other people, maybe they'd think a little harder about what they say *before* they say it.

"Is it your shoes?" Coach Mac says.

"A little pain is all," I say. I gesture in the general direction of my legs.

Coach Mac tilts her head. "You let yourself recover yesterday?"

I shrug but don't answer. Benny's walking by. He glances at me before speeding away.

Coach Mac narrows her eyes. She blows her whistle for the next group. I'm there when she says, "Good one, Natalie. Better than the last. Just over seventy seconds."

My heart hammers. I haven't broken seventy-three today. I really am slow.

Coach Mac turns back to me. "Why don't you sit the next few out, Leta? And we'll see if you can come back fresh."

But I'm already lined up at the starting line, and when she blows the whistle, I run.

Listen.

Maybe running won't change anything.

But if there's the slightest slim possibility that it will, I will keep running.

Coach Mac is mad.

She doesn't like any of us defying her orders, and she ordered me to sit a few out. Now she says, "On the bench for the rest of practice, Leta." She has the kind of eyes that say, *Don't you dare get back on the line.*

I don't dare get back on the line. I sit.

It's hard not to feel sorry for myself while I'm sitting. Coach Mac usually punishes us for our rebellion by adding more intervals to our workouts. She runs us until we can't run anymore so we learn our lesson and "listen to the person who knows the most about running on this track." She was a professional runner way back when. She ran the eight hundred. Like, almost went to the Olympics. And she *did* compete in the Olympics for some long-distance race. I don't remember which one.

She probably knows more about running than any of the other coaches, too, but they don't bother asking her opinion on anything. I'd like to say I don't know why, but I think I do. Coach Mac is a woman, and they're all men.

I watch the girls fly by, Natalie right there with them.

Nineteen

MONDAY

"Wait up, Leta!"

I turn and see Raina jogging toward me. I don't know how she has any energy or power left in her legs if she was working her hardest.

But she doesn't have anything to prove like I do. So she doesn't need to work her hardest on four-hundred-meter repeat days. The four hundred isn't her race. Coach Mac just makes us all do four-hundred-meter repeats because it helps build endurance, even for a short race like Raina's.

Chrissy joins us halfway to the bus stop. All three of us watch Sabrina climb into her mom's shiny white Suburban and Natalie pull herself into a giant black truck with wheels as high as my chest.

We don't talk about Sabrina or Natalie.

Instead, Raina says, "Are you okay?"

Chrissy adds, "You looked like you were limping there at the end."

My shins hurt so badly it's hard to walk normally. Coach Mac eventually let me get back on the line but also told me more than once that I could sit more intervals out if I wanted. I pretended like I didn't hear her. No one gets better sitting out.

And maybe it felt good to punish my body with pain.

It doesn't feel good now.

"I'm okay," I say. My voice sounds thick, and I try to swallow whatever's caught there.

They don't know how close I am to losing everything. And I'm not about to tell them.

Who would understand?

Raina and Chrissy still have their dads, even if Raina's makes her live with his mom and Chrissy's can't work because of a bad back. They don't have to prove anything to their dads, like I do.

Some things are impossible to explain. So I don't even try.

"That was a tough practice," Raina says as we settle into our bus seats.

"I hate the four hundred," Chrissy says. "I'm glad I only have one every track meet. I don't know how you run them all the time. My legs feel like warm Jell-O."

Raina laughs. "I can't even feel mine."

This feels like a conversation we've had before, the last time we did four-hundred-meter repeats. I don't have anything new to say.

I stare out the window.

I wish I couldn't feel my legs. But even sitting down, the pain throbs through the front of them.

If I can't run, Natalie will take my place. If I can't run, I'll lose before I've even had the chance to try.

If I can't run, I'll never fix things for Amelia.

I rub the front of my legs and will the pain away.

But there's a deeper pain, right in the center of my chest, and I don't think anything will make it go away.

Eight four hundreds and not one of them matched Natalie's time. Eight four hundreds and not one single lap without the needles that turned into nails. Eight four hundreds, the extra pain that kept perfect pace, and I still can't forget that face on the photo.

Why did Dad look so stupidly happy when he's not here with us?

Mom's not waiting when the bus pulls up to my stop. Pop usually picks me up on Mondays, but this morning Mom said, "I'm not working late today, so I'll be there to get you after practice."

Pop's always here when I step off the bus. She should have just let him come.

Mr. Meinke says, "You want me to wait?"

He still has to drive to Francitas and drop off the rest of the track kids. Their parents would worry if they were late.

So I say, "She'll be here," trying to pretend it doesn't bother me that she's not already.

She should be.

She should already be here.

She should already be here waiting.

When the bus pulls away and I'm alone, the attack starts in my legs. Not pain. A weakening. I grope the stone wall of the post office. One arm goes numb, and my vision starts to tunnel.

I can't breathe.

"She'll be here," I say out loud to myself. Sometimes it helps saying the words out loud.

But inside, words stick on repeat.

What if

What if

What if

I don't want to finish what's on the other end of the "what if"—because that might make it come true.

One bad thing happens, and a cascade of them come racing your way. You learn to expect that when you live lives like ours.

I stare in the direction of home.

Maybe she's not coming.

Maybe she forgot.

Maybe she's dead.

Maybe I should start walking myself home.

I swallow hard, and just as I limp across the gravel parking lot toward the highway, I see the speck of a car way in the distance. I make a bargain with whoever runs the world.

Let that be her, and I'll give Amelia that shirt she's always wanting to wear.

I blink hard and wait. If it's not Mom, I'll start walking home.

It's her.

After the relief practically buckles my legs again, anger moves in, fiery and fast.

Mom skids to a stop, gravel popping under her tires. "Sorry I'm late," she calls through the open window. The air-conditioning must not be working again. "You weren't worried, were you?"

I look out the window and blink hard again. "No." My voice still sounds thick and a little wobbly.

I know Mom sees through my act when she says, "I'm sorry, baby. I got a late start."

Amelia sulks in the back seat. The late start was probably because of her.

I try not to hold that against her.

Twenty

TUESDAY

The next day, my shins aren't hurting anymore, but my foot feels like someone battered it with a hammer during the night. Pain blazes through me every time I step on it. I wince and try my best not to limp. Maybe it just needs a little time to stretch out after sleeping all night.

But my foot's never needed time to stretch out.

Something's wrong, my brain yells. I tell it to shut up.

I wiggle my toes, take a deep breath, and move one step forward.

Pain slices like it's made of a thousand knives. I feel like the Little Mermaid, from the real fairy tale. I would never choose this for love.

I glare at my foot. *Don't you do this to me*, I tell it in my mind. There's too much depending on my feet. They need to work!

"What's wrong with your foot?" Amelia says. For once she's not asleep in our closet. The day I'd like her to be. Figures.

"Nothing," I say. "Just worry about yourself. You're not gonna make us late again."

"I didn't make us late yesterday," Amelia says, her voice pinched and annoyed. She's not a morning person.

"Yeah, well."

Does she need reminding of how many times she's made us late? I don't even think I can count the number of mornings we've had to sprint out to the bus, seconds away from being left behind.

I straighten my back and challenge myself to walk to the bathroom without limping. I make it all the way to the corner and out of Amelia's sight before the strain makes tears leak out my eyes.

What if my foot doesn't get better before the district meet?

What if it doesn't get better before today's practice, when I have to prove I'm still the fastest runner on the team, even with Natalie Dash added to the roster?

My foot isn't better at practice.

All day long, I've tried walking without a limp, the pain-tears so close I could hardly see anything through the massive blur my vision has become.

Just a couple of hours and then I can go home and ice it. I'll just tell Mom it's a little sore and hope that Pop isn't there to see through the lie.

He will be, though. He's the one picking me up today.

"Get moving, ladies," Coach Mac says. The first lap is supposed to be a warm-up, but sometimes Coach Mac gets impatient if we take too much time with it. I usually lead the pack and set the pace, but I guess I was going too slow.

I speed up a little, more knives joining the always-there ones in my foot. I'm relieved when we sit down to stretch out our legs.

At least, until I catch Natalie looking at me.

Does she see the weakness? Does she know what it means?

I wait for her to smile, to know she's won before we've even begun to run, but instead she drops her eyes to the ground and blinks hard.

And for some reason, it makes me hate her a little less. And maybe a little more, too.

Look, I know how ridiculously unreasonable it is to hate Natalie when I don't know a thing about her except that she runs track and is fast at the four hundred. Does she make good grades? I don't know. Does she like pizza? I've never asked. How many brothers and sisters does she have? I have no clue.

It's not fair that I hate her just because she runs my race. I'm the first one who will tell you that. And I'm not proud of myself either. Looking at Natalie, apart from all the rest of us, where we keep her just because she's new, makes me mad at myself and ashamed for the way I feel. It's not fair to hate or even dislike a person before you've given them a chance.

But the thing is, when you have so little, you get to where you're terrified of losing what little you have.

So I hate her because if she takes the four hundred from me, I will have nothing left.

Nothing left to prove I matter. That I'm not just another forgettable girl in a patriarchal world.

Some people are good at all sorts of things, but they're never really great at any one of them. They're what Mom calls "generalists." Dip a toe in here, dip another there.

I used to be like that. Until I found track.

If I can't be the best, who am I?

Coach Mac claps her hands and blows her whistle once. It's our cue to head toward the starting line.

Today we're running twelve two hundreds.

I've never liked the two hundred—not enough distance to settle into a pace—but Coach Mac says they're as good for me as they are for Raina.

We run the first one as another warm-up, to get our legs under us, as Coach Mac says. I listen for Natalie's time before walking back to the starting line.

I want to know it so I can beat it.

The pain is now a constant throb, but as soon as Coach Mac blows her whistle, I shove it deep, deep down, and I run.

I beat Natalie's time eleven times.

But by the end, my foot hurts so badly I can hardly walk off the track.

I feel Natalie's eyes on me. When I glance at her, her face looks pained.

Is she hurt, too?

I don't think so. Because when I'm almost out of the gate and into the parking lot where the bus waits, she says,

"You should rest your foot if it hurts. It won't get better running on it."

I don't know exactly what comes over me, but I turn on her. "You would love that, wouldn't you? It would open up a nice space for you to slide right in."

It's the meanest thing I've ever said to someone. She blinks at me, opens her mouth, and closes it again.

I watch her walk away, my insides hurting almost as much as my foot.

No one even tells her good-bye.

Twenty-one

TUESDAY

Raina and Chrissy talk practically nonstop on the bus ride home.

Sometimes I get my fill of words and all I want is quiet, but they're the kind of people who never get tired of words.

I listen to them talk about practice and Sabrina.

"Why do you think she stopped hanging out with us?" Raina says.

Chrissy shrugs. "I guess she found some better friends."

Raina rolls her eyes. "Briana and Brooke, you mean. Not exactly great friends."

"Cheerleaders," Chrissy says. "Like her. Cooler than us."

I haven't told them about the lists I found last week or the things Briana and Brooke said. I keep my mouth shut now, too.

Then Raina says, "The new girl's pretty fast."

Chrissy nods. They both look at me out of the corners of their eyes, but they don't look long. "I wonder what Coach will have her run," Chrissy says.

"Probably the four hundred," I say. I stare at the black slats on the floor. We're almost to Raina's stop.

"Well, she's not faster than you," Chrissy says. She sounds like she's trying to convince herself.

But I can't help but think, *Maybe I'm faster than her on a good day, but what about on a bad day, the kind of day a foot hurts so bad you can hardly walk on it, the kind of day you realize you can make every kind of plan in the world, prepare for every possible situation, but the universe or god or whatever you want to call it is still in charge? And you might have to sit out the biggest race of the season?*

I won't. No one can make me. My body, my choice, just like Mom always tells me.

Pop waits in the lot of the post office today. I grit my teeth and try to walk normally to his car. If he suspects I'm hurt, he'll tell Mom. And she'll make me sit out, and I can't sit out when I have to get faster.

"There's my runner girl," Pop says. I try not to look relieved when I sit down, but I sure am glad to get off my foot.

Tonight I plan to do as little walking as I possibly can. Maybe after some ice and elevation and rest, it'll feel good as new in the morning.

"How many four hundreds today?" Pop says. The tires of his tiny car squeal as he pulls onto the highway, and I swear we tip over to the right a little. I grip my door handle and try not to make the same noise as the tires.

"Two hundreds today. Twelve of them."

Pop shakes his head. "I still don't know why they have you running those things."

Pop thinks Coach Mac should train us more with distance. Two, three, or four miles on the track once or twice a week, he says, could build up our endurance as much as those sprints.

He's not a coach, so I don't really know who's right.

I shrug. "It wasn't so bad."

If my foot could talk, it would tell a much different story.

"Where's Amelia?" I say as soon as we walk into the house. I didn't even notice she wasn't in the car with us until we were halfway home. I was too preoccupied with my foot. And she's usually quiet when she's not sighing loudly or grumbling about how much she wishes she could stay home alone.

Maybe I did notice she wasn't there, but my brain filed it away as *Pop probably gave her another chance to prove she could be trusted at home alone. He's hopeful like that.*

"At a friend's." Pop jabs a thumb behind him, toward the other house that shares this driveway. It's way nicer than ours, all brick with big windows cut out of the front. I don't know why they hid it behind this falling-apart one.

I frown at Pop. Amelia's not supposed to go anywhere when Mom isn't home.

Pop seems to read my thought. He says, "She said your mom gave her permission."

Huh. I'll have to ask Mom tonight. I don't think the rules have changed. Amelia's only a fourth grader—not old enough to walk alone to a friend's, no matter how close that house is.

I glance back at the brick house where Amelia's supposed to be. You hardly ever see the parents of the four kids who live there. Does Mom even know them?

"Maybe I should go get her," I say.

Pop puts a hand on my shoulder just before I leap off the porch. It's a good thing, too. If my foot can't handle running, it sure can't handle jumping.

Pop nods in the direction of the house. Amelia walks toward us, eyes fixed on the gravel path. And even though she moves like the thick molasses Mom used to buy to sweeten our oatmeal, back before it was more than five dollars a bottle, we wait for her on the porch. When she's close enough to hear me, I can't help but say, "You really supposed to be at a friend's house?"

Amelia glares at me. "I didn't know I had two moms," she says.

I squeeze my fists. Pop's hand presses into my shoulder again. "Now, now, girls," he says. "Let's go inside and have us a nice supper. No good conversation comes from being hangry."

I follow Pop and Amelia inside, but now my thoughts have shifted to: *A nice supper with what?*

Mom's grocery trip Sunday didn't last long. Probably because of Amelia. I haven't eaten much besides dinner and an orange for breakfast yesterday and today.

Here's my inventory, the last time I checked—this morning, three days from payday:

The pantry had one can of Spam (so Mom does buy them on purpose, ew!), one can of red kidney beans, some old stale plain Cheerios (who knows how old, because Pop must have brought them over, and his house is where cereal goes to die), a plastic container of white sugar, a half-empty box of baking soda, one box of Hamburger Helper (which is probably what Mom plans for tonight's or tomorrow night's supper, even though we don't have any hamburger meat left), some brown lunch bags, and a broom.

The refrigerator had a small package of carrots on their way to getting bendy, two leftover potatoes, a jar with two olives floating in cloudy juice, a mostly full bottle of Gatorade (the green kind I can't stand), an old jar of mayonnaise, a new jar of Miracle Whip, an almost-gone bottle of ketchup, a jar of relish, some lunch meat that's starting to curl up at the edges, a leftover container of last night's Hamburger Helper, and a salad so brown and soupy it looked like it might've been gathered from a sewage stream. Mom must have bought the clearance salad when she went on Sunday. We just didn't eat it fast enough.

The freezer had an almost-empty bag of Mom's Hershey's Kisses, a box with one corn dog left, a half-empty bag of flour, and a container full of ice because Mom gets really mad if we don't fill it or the ice trays after we help ourselves to ice.

Using even the most creative parts of my imagination, I can't create a nice supper out of what's left.

"Well," Pop says after he's done his own inventory like I did this morning, "we'll figure something out." He shoos us out of the kitchen, but he doesn't say anything about picking something up. That's probably because he doesn't have any more money either.

You get used to figuring something out when you live paycheck to paycheck.

Pop does figure something out. By the time Mom comes home, there's a stack of cheeseless bean quesadillas (mostly tortillas, since there was only one can of beans). We each get two, with a few extra leftover tortillas—which aren't as good as Chrissy's mom's tortillas but are good enough for me.

And even though Pop says these quesadillas have pieces of Spam in them, too, I clean my plate.

Running makes you hungry, remember?

Amelia and I are already in bed when we hear Mom and Pop talking.

Maybe they don't realize how far their voices travel in such a small house, but with the right kind of breathing and your head turned toward the door, you can hear just about everything that happens inside these walls.

"Still no money from him, huh?" Pop says.

"Nothing's changed in three days, Dad," Mom says. She sounds either exhausted or annoyed. Maybe both.

It's been more than three days, but who cares about technicalities? Pop doesn't.

"You know there are programs—"

"We've already talked about this," Mom says. "I'm not getting on food stamps. We'll be all right." A pause. "I get paid on Friday. The girls get lunch at school."

I hope Amelia gets lunch at school. I hope they don't look at her there like they look at me in the junior high lunch line. Or, if they do, I hope she doesn't care.

I don't know why I care. I know it's stupid to care. And it's hard to explain. It's just . . . you feel like you're doing something wrong, I guess. Like you should be ashamed of yourself for being in a position where your parents can't pay for your school lunch. Even though it's not your fault. And it's not even your parents' fault, or at least not your mom's, but they look at you like it's *your* fault and her fault and his fault and everybody in your family's fault. Like your parents are shameful people and you're a shameful person and the world is better off without all of you.

You know what it's like living with those kinds of eyes looking at you every time you have to eat?

Maybe that's why Mom doesn't want to get on food

stamps. Maybe she'd have eyes like that looking at her every time she went through the checkout line at the store.

"The girls still have to eat tomorrow night and Thursday night," Pop says. Like Mom doesn't know. I wish he'd just let it go. She doesn't need this kind of stress on top of all the other stress. I know he's trying to look out for us, but Mom's doing the best she can. I know he knows that.

People say all kinds of things when they're scared. And I guess that's what scares me: that Pop and Mom are both scared too. How will this turn out? How long will she let it go? When will Dad remember his responsibility? Remember us?

"I'll figure it out, Dad." Mom sounds angry. I understand why, but I want to tell her not to be angry with Pop. As far as I know, he's only ever wanted to help. And he's helped the best he can.

But maybe she's not really mad at Pop. Maybe she's mad at Dad, and the anger doesn't care about who's to blame.

I know that just as well as anyone, don't I?

I wasn't really mad at Natalie. But my words sure sounded like I was.

My insides do their little twisting dance again, and I try to swallow the shame.

But some things are easier to swallow than others. Some things have thorns and spikes and blades, and they tear all the way down.

Twenty-two

WEDNESDAY

Last night Mom said the *D* word.

Amelia and I had already done our good night rituals, in whispers this time, when we heard Mom say, "Turns out a divorce is more expensive than I thought."

Pop had gone home. She was talking to someone on the phone. Maybe her sister, maybe a friend. It didn't matter who.

I practically stopped breathing.

Divorce? How was I supposed to get Dad to come back home, give Amelia that perfect daddy-daughter dance, if Mom was already giving up and considering a divorce?

My anger surprised me.

It took a long time to fall asleep.

And when Mom shook me awake this morning, it

surprised me that my anger was still there, pointed right at her.

I didn't say a word to her, not even "I love you," before she walked out the door.

Look, I know it's not Mom's fault that the *D* word showed up.

I guess I just thought we had a little more time to win Dad back. To change his heart, his mind, his whole self. To prove we were worth sticking around for . . . or maybe just to prove *I* was worth sticking around for.

Divorce takes all my hopes and shreds them up under track-shoe-spiked feet.

"Get up, Amelia!" I shake Amelia for the third time. This time she's fallen asleep in her kitchen chair, a bowl of those leftover stale Cheerios beside her head. No milk included.

How does she sleep in a chair that hard?

"Okay!" Amelia says, her voice still groggy.

"I shouldn't have to get you up more than once." Maybe I'm in a bad mood this morning. Maybe I'm taking all my anger out on Amelia now. Maybe I know this, but I'm powerless to stop it, because more words fly out. "I shouldn't have to be your second mom."

"I didn't ask you to be my second mom!" Amelia says. She sounds angry now too.

"You didn't have to," I say.

Amelia storms out the front door, her backpack still on the floor beside her chair.

I sigh, pick up the backpack, and follow her out.

Mrs. Crisp asks me before class how my letter project is going. I knew I should have hidden in the bathroom instead of coming to class early.

The truth is, I haven't written a thing. I don't usually have a hard time with my writing assignments, but for some reason this one feels impossible. Maybe it's because I've stopped believing letters can change anything.

How many letters did I write to Dad over the years? And he never came home. He never even wrote back.

I manage to mumble a "Fine" without it sounding too much like a lie.

Mrs. Crisp smiles at me. "I'm sure you'll do a fantastic job with the assignment. You always do."

I hate to disappoint her. I turn away and head toward my seat.

"Your foot okay?"

Mrs. Crisp's words make me wince almost as much as putting weight on my foot. I'll have to concentrate on walking without a limp so Coach Mac doesn't see. At least it's Wednesday, which is a stretching and yoga day in athletics.

I toss Mrs. Crisp another "Fine" without looking at her. I know I'm being rude. And it's completely unlike me, which means Mrs. Crisp is probably wondering and will probably ask what's bothering me.

She doesn't get the opportunity before two of Sabrina's new cheerleader friends come in, heading to the back of the room. They stare at me, and I want to tell them to take a picture, it will last longer. But it's mean, and Mrs. Crisp is still watching.

It's not who I am, and I know that.

"Good," Mrs. Crisp says, continuing our conversation even though there are observers now. "I hear you have a big race coming up."

A big race I'll probably lose.

Why does it feel like everywhere I look I'm just a big disappointment to people?

At lunch Chrissy and Raina sit on the same side of the table and stare me down.

"What?" I say.

"We've noticed your limp," Chrissy says.

"I don't have a limp," I say.

Raina gives me the kind of look that says, *Do we look stu-*

pid or something? "What's going on with your foot?"

"Nothing," I say.

"Something," Chrissy says.

"It's just a little sore is all. From practice yesterday. I think my period's coming up."

That's not a lie. I'm in the luteal phase, the week before my period's supposed to start. Coach Mac says that's when inflammation in the body is highest, so we have to be careful not to stress it too much and cause injury.

Raina and Chrissy know all about the phases of our periods, like me, because Coach Mac talks about them *all the time*. They know that the luteal phase is when the body feels achy and bloated and out of sorts. But they completely ignore what I've said.

"You think you should run in Saturday's meet?" Raina says. She glances at Chrissy, and I know what she's thinking: If I don't race in this week's meet, the new girl might claim my spot on the mile relay.

And in the four hundred—but she's probably not as worried about that.

Sabrina's the slowest out of the four of us on the relay team. Coach Mac wouldn't take me off.

Would she?

My throat feels dry when I say, "I'll be fine. Don't worry."

It's the only option, so it has to be true.

Twenty-three

WEDNESDAY

All day long I try to minimize the pressure on my foot, save whatever it has left for practice. But even still, during our warm-up lap, the pain knifes through the center of my foot. Apparently yoga and stretching in athletics class didn't help *at all*.

I'm angry at yoga. It's supposed to be miraculous.

We're doing a ladder workout today. We start with a pair of one hundreds, move up to two hundreds, then four hundreds, then six hundreds and all the way back down. The rests between the intervals get shorter as we go.

I have to work extra hard not to limp during the rests. I shake out my foot, rub it, stretch it when Coach Mac isn't looking. When she is looking, I grit my teeth and try my best to run as hard as I always have.

But I get tired. The pain starts consuming me. After a while it's impossible not to limp the tiniest bit.

"Leta!" Coach Mac calls after the first four hundred.

I try to jog across six lanes, but the pain reminds me to walk. I know Coach Mac is watching me close, so I try my hardest not to let on how agonizing every step is.

"Your foot bothering you again?" she says. Her voice is quiet, like maybe she doesn't want anyone else to hear. Sabrina and Callie walk toward the starting line. Coach Mac blows her whistle, and the six lined up take off. Coach Mac didn't even give them time to recover. Their breaths sounded so heavy they could have been the wind blowing in a cool front—and that was before they started running this interval.

"Just a little sore," I say.

Coach Mac looks at me like she doesn't believe me. "Where's it hurt?"

I shrug.

Everywhere.

I keep my mouth shut.

"One place or all over?" Coach Mac says.

If I wanted her to know, I could point out the exact place I feel the knife—right between my second and third toes. But I shrug and say, "Hard to say. All over?" Because maybe that's better than pain in one place.

Coach Mac sighs. "Why don't you sit out the rest of practice." It's not a question or a request. It's an order.

My heart drops all the way to my feet. And it doesn't need to be there, because it makes the pain so much worse!

"No." The word rises up and twists out of me, like something wild and thorny, like maybe that one word holds all my anger and all my resentment and all my fear and all my sadness and everything else I could possibly feel about the last week of my life.

Coach Mac blinks at me. Maybe she's never had anyone argue with her. Probably that's it. She's very fierce.

She folds her arms across her chest. "I'm not letting you run on an injured foot. It's irresponsible."

"It's fine." My words are half wail, half plea.

Coach Mac shakes her head. "It's not gonna kill you to take the rest of the day off."

But how do you get faster if you can't run your race? So I take off running, the searing pain a reminder of why this matters so much.

Sometimes you have to break to put things back together.

The best runs are the ones where you feel weightless, like instead of legs, you have wings, like instead of ground, you race on clouds.

The best runs are the ones where your body can't feel feet, calves, thighs, hamstrings, hip flexors, all the little aches and burns and numbing, but instead it feels only the warm satisfaction of lungs pulling in air, pushing it back out, pulling, pushing, pulling, pushing, in the kind of rhythm that feels effortless.

The best runs are the ones where you forget you're running and your mind instead bends around imaginary worlds or hopes or dreams or pretend conversations that end exactly the way you want them to: happily ever after.

The best runs are the ones where you forget yourself, the pain in your foot, the impossibility of finishing strong when you've never felt so weak.

This is not one of those runs.

"Hey!"

Someone runs beside me.

Natalie.

We've coming up on the last curve.

I run harder, pain making it almost impossible to see. There's a blackness edging my vision, growing bigger with every step.

"Those things don't just go away!" Natalie yells into the air around us. "You need to stop running."

Like I would ever stop running when she's here beside me. Coach Mac sent the wrong person if she was trying to get me to quit.

I will never ever quit.

I pick up the pace as much as I can. And maybe Natalie knows I won't stop until I beat her, because a few steps from the finish line she pulls up short, stops completely, and lets me cross it alone.

It doesn't feel like a victory, though, especially when I see Coach Mac's face.

"Leta Laurel!" Coach Mac's eyes blaze. "You sit your butt down on this bench, and you do not move again."

I've never seen Coach Mac so angry before. The girls stare. Raina's mouth drops open. Chrissy gives me the kind of look that says, *I would not trade places with you for a whole bag of Mami's dulce de leche candy.* Her mom makes the best dulce de leche candy, too.

Sabrina turns away, but not before I see the smirk on her face.

Anger blazes into my chest again. Makes the world a giant blur. Hollows out the wound and squeezes so tight it starts throbbing. Coach Mac's whistle shrills from a thousand miles away.

Before practice is over, Coach Mac calls me, Sabrina, Raina, and Chrissy to the stretching area, where the high jump mat is set up.

She tells us she's changed up the relay team, and my heart starts thrashing like I finished the entire ladder workout, same as everyone else here, instead of sitting my butt on the bench.

But then she says, "Leta, you're still the anchor," and I let loose all the anxiety trapped in my chest. It sounds like a gust of summer wind.

Raina's moved to the third leg, Chrissy the second, and Natalie's the new first leg.

Sabrina's eyes flash, but she doesn't say anything. Coach Mac says, "Sabrina, you'll be the alternate in case someone gets sick." She glances my direction. "Or injured."

I almost tell her my foot will definitely be fine by Saturday, but I decide it's probably best not to tempt fate.

I head toward the late bus, but Coach Mac calls me back. She runs a hand through her short black hair before saying,

"Leta, I want you to take it easy on that foot if it's hurting you. I'd rather have you for district than this weekend's meet."

"Okay," I say.

"I mean it," Coach Mac says. "That little stunt you pulled could have done more damage."

I look at my foot and bite my lip. The pain doesn't feel any different. It's still the same giant loud.

"Sometimes you have to sit out a race to run the ones that matter," Coach Mac says.

But Coach Mac doesn't understand. Every race matters. They all get me one step closer to being the kind of girl a person can never forget.

Even a dad with a brand-new life and girlfriend.

Round 3

Amelia smirks at me from the chair.

She's expecting a fight. And while it would feel nice to put my foot up in the recliner with a bag of ice strapped to it, I just pass her by. Limping. I hear her gasp.

I don't feel like explaining.

And when she calls out, "What's wrong with you?" I don't answer.

Nothing's wrong with me, I tell myself. *Nothing at all.*

If you tell yourself something often enough, maybe eventually you believe it.

Twenty-four

WEDNESDAY

Mom's late getting home.

It's already dark. Pop left an hour ago, after picking me up from the bus stop and dropping me off here. He doesn't usually pick me up on Wednesdays, but Mom called to say she was working a little later than usual and would be home at seven.

He seemed distracted the whole time, so he didn't notice my limp.

I'm glad. If he tells Mom, she'll take me to the doctor, who might want X-rays, and all that's more money than we have to spare. Not to mention, if a doctor tells me I can't run in a race, Mom will make sure I don't run in the race.

I pace in front of the double windows of the dining

room, back and forth, back and forth. Heat climbs up my arm and into my chest. My throat swells and makes it harder to breathe than an all-out mile.

I already fed Amelia the last box of Hamburger Helper, without the hamburger. It was actually better without the hamburger.

"Mom's late," Amelia says, stating the obvious.

I don't say anything. I lift one of the plastic blinds and squint, hoping I see headlights in the distance.

I don't.

It's getting harder and harder to breathe. She should have called if she was going to be late. I think about calling her cell phone. But what if she doesn't answer? Or what if she's driving and her phone rings and she gets into an accident and...

I feel Amelia's eyes on me. I turn away. "She'll be home soon," Amelia says.

I wish I could have Amelia's certainty. I wish I could swallow this panic. I wish I could ignore the words that twist round and round in my head.

What if she doesn't come home?

What if something happened to her?

What if we lost the only parent who remembers we're alive?

What if the last thing I said to her was not "I love you" but absolutely nothing?

I head out the front door and leave Amelia standing at the table.

I'm almost to the end of the driveway, forgetting my vow to stay off my feet for the rest of the night, when I see a car pull onto our road, miles away. I stand in the ditch, watching, until I'm sure it's Mom because it doesn't turn into the driveways of any of the other houses sprinkled along our road.

Only then do I turn around and limp back to the house. Her tires pop on gravel before I reach the porch.

Mom's first words to me are "Sorry. Had some last-minute shipments come in. I had to help unload them."

I don't tell her she could've called to let us know. I don't tell her I was worried sick. I don't tell her about my panic attack or my foot or the disappointing practice today.

And she doesn't ask.

It's like we're miles and miles apart, even when we're in the same room.

Twenty-five

THURSDAY

As soon as I line up with all the others to jog the first lap and do our stretches, Coach Mac says, "Leta, come here. Everyone else can go ahead and get started."

But I'm the pacesetter.

It's okay, I tell myself. *I'll catch up.*

But Coach Mac says, "You're not running today, Leta."

"What?"

Coach Mac looks down at my foot, then back up at me. "You think I haven't noticed how bad that foot is hurting you?"

I at least thought I was hiding it well.

"You need to rest," Coach Mac says. "And if you can't make yourself do it, then I will."

"I'll rest tomorrow." Fridays are our day off, not Thursdays.

"You'll rest today," Coach Mac says, one hand on a hip. She points to a bench beside the finish line, where she stands with her stopwatch. "Now sit down."

I blink hard and try to steady myself. "But how am I supposed to win a race without training for it?" Tears are folded and stuffed inside my words, and I know Coach Mac can hear them.

She sits down next to me. The mob of runners is only halfway around the track. They're going way slower than they would if I was leading them. Or maybe not. I'm pretty slow right now too. "You've had enough training." She watches the mob float around the last curve. "Besides." She stands. "We're doing something different today."

I feel Raina's and Chrissy's eyes on me as they pass, but I don't look at them.

If I do, I'll cry.

I watch Natalie run six two hundreds and six one hundreds before Coach Mac blows her whistle and waves everybody toward the high jump area. I don't know if I'm supposed to come, too, until Coach Mac says, "Come on, Leta."

She tells us all to have a seat. She sits down, too, her long legs folded up underneath her.

Coach Mac looks at all of us without speaking, like she's waiting for some kind of confession. A couple of girls shift. Someone clears her throat. The silence feels heavy and uncomfortable.

"I wanted to spend the rest of today's practice doing some team building," Coach Mac finally says.

Team building? We've never done anything like this before.

"You're all runners," Coach Mac continues. "Running your own race. Sometimes that makes you forget you're a team. That we're all in this together."

She lets the words settle around us for half a minute or so. I don't know what the other girls are thinking, but I can't help but think about Natalie and how most of us haven't even given her a chance.

"I know most of you have been running two-hundred-yard dashes since elementary, when everyone got a purple participation ribbon," Coach Mac says. I got three of them before I actually started winning. "But we have a new teammate now. Someone who hasn't run with you all your lives."

I sneak a look at Natalie. She stares at the ground, her cheeks pink.

Coach Mac says, "I don't want any of you to forget, at the end of the day, no matter which race you run or how fast you are or whether you gave it your all . . ." She pauses. "We are still a team. We look out for each other. Care about each other. Know each other."

I don't know what exactly Coach Mac has in mind, but I can tell it's important to her. So I say, "Like a family."

Coach Mac's eyes meet mine. "Yes, Leta. Like a family."

And I think, *Well, families can be screwed up too.*

And that makes me wonder, *How can we make sure this one isn't?*

My eyes wander to Sabrina. She doesn't look back at me.

Coach Mac says, "Let me tell you about the bonobos."

"The bonobos?" Brooke says. Briana giggles, even though there's not really anything to giggle about. They exchange a look that seems to say, *Coach Mac is so weird*, or something stupid like that.

How do you make sure your family isn't screwed up with people like them in it?

I almost immediately feel bad for thinking that. Because it's not much of a family thing to think, either, is it? I guess we're all just trying to figure out who we are and where we belong.

"The bonobos are great apes that live in the Congo Basin," Coach Mac says. Someone snorts. I'm pretty sure

Brooke or Briana—or maybe both—was the snorter.

I'm trying to follow along, but what's the Congo Basin? Someone asks. I think it's Callie.

"The Congo Basin is in Central Africa," Coach Mac says. Brooke and Briana make the same kind of face, like, *Why are we talking about great apes in Central Africa?* I want to tell them if they just wait a few minutes, I'm sure Coach Mac will tell us.

And she does. She says, "The bonobos have a unique way of living." She glances at each one of us as she talks. "Female bonobos protect one another, whether they know one another or like one another or are related to one another."

"Protect one another from what?" Raina says.

Mean girls, I want to say. I keep my mouth shut, because there's fire inside me, sparking and twitching, and I don't want to burn down everything Coach Mac is trying to build.

"Male aggression," Coach Mac says. "But also everything else."

I still don't think I'm understanding, really. Is she saying we should protect one another from boys? And what boys do? What do boys do?

I think of the lists from the last track meet and how Brooke and Briana and Sabrina laughed about them because they weren't on the terrible ones, only the ones they considered good or flattering or whatever. Is that what Coach

Mac is talking about? Does she even know about the lists? The thought that she does makes my face heat up.

"The most important thing about the bonobos is they're a sisterhood," Coach Mac says. "They look out for their sisters. They stand up for their sisters. They form alliances instantly and without question." She pauses, and I wonder if everyone else is thinking about Natalie and how we've sort of treated her like an outsider. Or am I the only one?

"And they understand they're not competing against one another, because they're a sisterhood," Coach Mac continues. She meets my eyes. "A team."

"But we *are* competing," Callie says. "We compete in our races."

"We do the best we can to cross that finish line first in our individual races," Coach Mac says. "But sometimes it's not our day. Sometimes it's someone else's day." She's looking at Chrissy now, who's beside me. "And we celebrate that it was their day. Because we're a sisterhood."

I'm not entirely sure how I feel about that. Celebrating someone else's win, which is your loss? How is that even possible? It seems like it takes a better person than me.

Coach Mac keeps going. "No one harms a sister, and everyone is welcome in the sisterhood." She stares us down. "Everyone."

"Even boys?" one of the girls calls out.

"Boys, girls, people who don't identify as either, people who identify as both," Coach Mac says. "Everyone." She lets the words sit for a second before continuing. "We don't judge each other. We don't tear each other apart. We don't laugh when one of us falls down." *Or gets put on a terrible list*, I add in my mind. "We build each other up and stand strong, together."

No one says a word.

"Nothing can stand against a sisterhood," Coach Mac says. "Not even hand-me-down uniforms from the boys' team." We laugh.

Coach Mac lifts her chin. "We are a bonobo sisterhood," she continues. "We cheer each other on, and we never stop defending each other." She sits back on her heels. "I want you all to think about that for a few minutes."

The boys pass on the track, their feet slapping out the seconds and minutes. I can't help but notice Brooke and Briana leaning their heads together, whispering, watching the boys. Probably not doing what Coach Mac has asked us to do.

How do you build a sisterhood when some seem uninterested in the founding principles?

I get what Coach Mac is saying, but some things are out of your control. Not everyone wants to be a sisterhood.

After a few minutes of silence, when we're supposed to be thinking about what she's told us and not watching the boys run, Coach Mac starts asking us questions. "How long have you been a runner?"

We all answer different things. "Couple of years." "All my life." "Since my mama threatened to spank me and I had to do something about it." It sounds funny, the way Katie says it, but most of us know it's no joke when Katie's mom hits her. She's come to school with bruised arms, black eyes, a wrist in a cast once. (It didn't stop her from running her race—the eight hundred.)

"What's the best thing about running?" Coach Mac says.

"Flying." "Thinking." "Leaving everything behind but the road and whatever music you have playing in your AirPods."

That last one is Sabrina's answer. She's the only one of us whose parents can afford AirPods for their kids. She looks embarrassed that she said it out loud. She presses a hand to her mouth. I get it. Only Raina and Chrissy and I know about what she wants to leave behind—a mom who constantly tells her she's had enough to eat, she'll get fat eating like that, has she weighed herself recently, she looks like she's putting on weight.

I guess I know some of Sabrina's secrets too.

"What's your favorite race?" Coach Mac says.

"The two hundred." "Four hundred." "Mile." "Whatever will get me out of the house the longest."

That's from Chrissy. Her parents fight a lot. And they're loud about it.

Coach Mac ends with the hardest question, the same one I couldn't answer when Pop asked me.

"Why do you run?"

Nobody says anything for a while until Heather and Tiffany, twins on the cheerleading squad, say, "To be thin." Coach Mac wrinkles her nose but doesn't say anything. "To win," Briana says. She runs the eight hundred, like Katie. She usually comes in second. Coach Mac tilts her head but still doesn't say anything.

When everybody's answered except Natalie and me, Coach Mac says, "What about you, Natalie? Why do you run?"

Natalie picks at something on the ground in front of her before lifting her eyes. "I run to be free."

I look at her. She meets my gaze for only a second before dropping her eyes back to her hands.

It feels true for me, too.

But then a question slides in: *Do I run to be free or to forget that I'm not?*

I don't have time to answer this question, because Coach Mac says, "Women in the sisterhood have run your race before you ever did. They stand with you on the starting line. And they run with you every step of the way."

I think about that. I'm not the first eighth-grade girl who has ever run the four hundred. And I'm not the last. And all the ones who have done it before will be right there with me when the starting gun goes off.

It's a nice thought.

And maybe it's true for life, too. The things we go through. Maybe I'm not the first forgettable eighth-grade girl whose dad doesn't bother to send money to help out with groceries and school clothes and track shoes. Maybe all the others who have lived that life stand with me and walk with me every step of the way. I'm not alone, no matter how alone I feel.

I guess that's the real power of a sisterhood.

We don't do any more running after that. Coach Mac dismisses us ten minutes early.

"Well, that was interesting," Chrissy says.

"What do you think about the sisterhood?" Raina says.

"I think it's pretty cool," Chrissy says.

"But I don't think everybody does," Raina says. She nods toward Briana and Brooke and Sabrina, who walk toward Sabrina's mom's Suburban.

"Well, it's their loss," Chrissy says. "*We* can be a sisterhood." She stops right where she is, which is the middle of the parking lot, and turns to face Raina and me. "Deal?" She holds out her pinkie, like we used to do when we were younger and sealed everything with a pinkie swear.

"Deal," Raina says, hooking her pinkie around Chrissy's.

"Deal," I say, hooking mine around both of theirs. Because it's what we've always been anyway. We've kept each other's secrets, we've defended each other against pretty much everything, we've built each other up and stood strong together. When Raina's mom came back and Raina thought it might be forever and then she left again and the hurt sliced through our friend. When Chrissy had to move into the trailer park after her dad lost his job and they never really recovered. When Sabrina's mom put her on a diet that included no pizza, no treats, and no bread at all, which pretty much sucked all the joy out of the world. When Dad stopped calling.

My chest squeezes. I look toward Sabrina, climbing into that big Suburban and waving to Brooke and Briana.

It was always the four of us. Now it's the three of us.

But maybe that's where it starts. Three become more. And before you know it, every girl at Lolita Junior High will be walking down the halls, knowing she's never alone.

It seems like that could change the world.

Pop picked up McDonald's on the way to get me.

I don't care much for the greasy burgers and fries, but Pop says, "Cheapest burgers around. Better than nothing." I know he probably spent his last dollars on food for me and Amelia, so I don't complain. Tomorrow's payday and Mom will be able to fill the fridge and pantry.

Hopefully.

Before he leaves us, Pop says, "You ready for the meet Saturday?"

He hasn't said anything about my foot, and I haven't offered any information. It's much better that he hasn't noticed my limp. Have I mentioned I'm a terrible liar? And usually that's a good thing, but sometimes you do need the skill.

"Yep," I say. I try to sound like I really am ready for the meet, but honestly I'm a little scared. What if my foot doesn't get better by then? District is a week from Saturday, and that doesn't leave much time to get faster.

This week's meet is three hours away, but Pop's going. That's the kind of grandpa he is.

Mom has book fair this week, and the elementary school decided Saturday would be a perfect day for families to attend. Before Mom knew about my meet, she volunteered to help out. So only Pop will be at my meet this week.

"Don't be late," I say.

It's a joke between us. Pop's never late. Mom, on the other hand . . .

Amelia eats the rest of my fries.

She hasn't said much of anything since my panic attack last night. I guess I haven't said much of anything to her, either, besides our good night ritual.

Maybe I'm a little embarrassed that my younger sister saw me like that, since I'm supposed to be strong and in control. And maybe she's still a little mad at me for acting like her mom.

We don't talk about these things. It's just easier not to.

Even though I should be making sure she's done her homework and packed up for school tomorrow, I let Amelia sit in front of the television, watching some prank video show on YouTube, until Mom comes home.

Sometimes I just don't have the energy to take care of anyone else but me.

Twenty-six

FRIDAY

The day flies.

My foot feels better—or at least that's what I tell myself when my limp gets a little less obvious. And I'll have the whole afternoon to rest it without Chrissy and Raina looking at me like they're worried I won't be able to run tomorrow.

I'll be able to run tomorrow.

I have to.

I will accept no other reality.

As soon as we get off the bus, Amelia takes off toward the house at the end of the driveway.

"Hey! Amelia! Where are you going?"

"To my friends'!" She only turns around long enough to toss the words in my direction.

"Stop!" I say.

She keeps running.

I can't run after her. I can't undo the progress I've made on healing my foot.

"Amelia!"

She's not supposed to go anywhere but home. But she's not listening or stopping.

So I do what I have to do.

I take off running after her.

I catch her fast, even though every other step feels like torture.

Maybe that's why I'm so angry when I grab her arm and spin her around. She may have cost me tomorrow's meet.

"You're not allowed to go to a friend's unless Mom's home." My words come out clenched between my teeth. I bet my face looks like a tornado's coming. That's how my insides feel, anyway.

But Amelia's face looks the same. She tries to shake off my hand, but I'm afraid she'll take off running again, and my foot won't survive another chase.

"Let me go!" she says.

"No. You're supposed to come right home. Lock the doors. Don't go outside. Don't answer the phone."

"It's like we're in prison," Amelia says.

It's how Mom keeps us safe when she can't be home. Why's Amelia acting like this? She's never challenged the rules before. I mean, not in such a dramatic way.

"I've been going over to Casey and Cassidy's house all week," Amelia says.

I knew Mom shouldn't have given Amelia another chance to stay home alone. She doesn't understand the importance of rules.

"Not today," I say. I turn back toward our house, pulling Amelia along with me. It's not hard. She weighs about as much as four of the grocery bags Mom brings home from the store. I try to pile them on my arms so I don't have to make as many trips to the car. Apparently I've trained for Dragging Amelia Home When She's Trying to Rebel.

Amelia slaps at my hand. "You're not my mom!" she yells.

"Mom's not here!" I yell back.

"I hate you!" she says. "You're the worst sister ever! The worst *person* ever! I wish you weren't my sister! I wish you'd go away and never come back!"

The words sink into my chest and open a hole.

I let her go. Amelia looks down at my hand, but she doesn't move. Her eyes are wild-looking.

Maybe I'm tired of playing Second Mom. I say, "Go, then. Play with your friends. See if I care."

Amelia looks at me for one more second, then spins around and races toward her friends' house.

She only looks back once.

It's weird being in an empty house. I wonder if that's why Amelia started going to Casey and Cassidy's house, even if it's against the rules.

I prop my foot up with an ice pack wrapped around it.

At least I have Dad's old chair to myself.

And a little peace and quiet.

Amelia comes home right before six. Mom will drive up soon, hopefully with supper and a trunk full of groceries.

I don't say anything to Amelia, even when she asks me what time Mom's supposed to get home. I shrug and pretend to keep reading.

But my mind's too scattered to read any words, even

though *Patina* is one of my favorite books. And not just because of track. Because Patina and I are so much alike.

A thousand thoughts tangle around each other.

What if I can't run in tomorrow's meet? What if it sets me back? What if I don't win district? What if I can't bring Dad back home and what if he never starts sending money to help us and what if we don't have enough to eat ever again?

How am I supposed to keep Amelia safe, give her what she needs, if I can't even run my race?

Mom does come home with groceries, but it's not as much as she usually brings home on payday. It's mostly Hamburger Helper, fish sticks, french fries, and some cans of chicken noodle soup and SpaghettiOs.

She looks so sorry about it, I don't say a word.

Mom knocks on the bathroom door.

I've been in here a while, going over and over my legs with a razor to make sure I don't miss any hair.

The only list I want to make this meet is Fastest Girl.

"Leta?" Mom says. "Everything okay in there?"

Mom's started checking on me lately if I stay too long in the bathroom. I've had my period since the summer, but she still thinks that's the explanation if I hide in here for more than twenty minutes or so. I guess she's just making sure I know everything I need to know. Which I appreciate most days.

"Yeah, Mom," I say. "Everything's fine."

I run the razor over both legs one more time, for good measure. The skin feels raw, but at least it's mostly smooth. Except for the irritated bumps I always get.

I sigh.

When I open the bathroom door and walk into the kitchen, Mom gives me a funny look. "What were you doing in there?"

I think about telling her I was pooping, which might get her off my case. But I'm too tired to do anything but tell the truth. "Shaving."

"I thought you weren't gonna shave anymore."

"Sometimes societal expectations win, Mom."

I guess I decided to be like everyone else. I don't say this part out loud, and Mom doesn't say anything either. She just looks at me like she feels sorry for me. Or she regrets something. Or . . . I don't know. It's hard to tell anymore.

But because I can feel her eyes on me, I try my best not to limp until I reach my room and close my door.

Maybe girls are only brave in bigger sisterhoods. Ones that have more than three people in them.

I can't stop thinking about those lists from the last meet. I shaved my legs and put baking soda in my shoes, but I can't do anything about being poor. So I'll probably be put on another list. It's not in my control. You know what that's like, not being able to control the terrible things some boys say about you? (I know it's not all boys. Just like not all girls are mean.)

The bonobos have it figured out. I wish humans could figure it out.

I also can't stop thinking about the way Brooke and Briana and Sabrina laughed like the lists had nothing to do with them. Like being part of a team isn't about looking out for each other and standing up for what's right.

In their position, what would I have done?

Twenty-seven

SATURDAY

Pop shows up before the sun's even started rising. I'm already waiting, an orange in my hand. Mom got up to tell me bye, good luck, run fast, love you, and went back to bed. Amelia didn't even move when I climbed over her to turn off the alarm.

"How's the foot?" Pop says when we're on our way. I guess he did notice.

I clear my throat. "What do you mean?" It's a pretty bad attempt to pretend nothing's wrong.

"You think I haven't noticed your limp?" Pop says. "What did you do to it, anyway?"

"It's just a little sore," I say. "Better today."

Pop looks at me out of the corner of his eye. "Don't run on it if it still hurts. Sometimes pain is our body telling us to take a break."

That sounds like something quitters say. I don't have time to rest. I have a race to run. To win.

I keep my mouth shut.

Pop drops me off at the school, where Coach Mac already has the bus running and waiting, lights inside blazing like she doesn't plan to let any of us sleep on the three-hour drive to the meet.

I feel a groan coming. It's a long way to Bloomington. That's some serious sleep time we'll be missing. Sleep is recovery. Doesn't she want us to recover?

I wish the meet were here. I run better on my own track. But the district meet isn't here either. I tell myself it's good to practice on an unfamiliar track so I'm ready for it.

Pop holds up a hand. "See you soon, Leta Lightning Laurel!" To Coach Mac he says, "Race you to the meet, Coach!"

Coach Mac rolls her eyes, but she's also smiling.

Everybody loves Pop.

He should be our mascot. He'd probably love that.

"Uniforms on, ladies," Coach Mac says.

We trudge into the locker room, which also has blazing lights. It's way too bright in here. I squint and fumble around with my uniform.

"How is it possible that these uniforms got smaller between last week and this one?" Raina says. The top is stretched across her boobs. "Ugh!" she groans.

"Just think of it like an extra sports bra," Chrissy says.

Raina shoves her. "Please. No one wants their chest on display while they're running."

She's right about that. I'm glad my uniform hangs off me. "Just try not to think about it," I say.

"Easier said than done," Raina says.

Chrissy's shorts ride up as we walk to the bus. She keeps tugging them down, but she has to do it every three steps. "I'd rather have a tight shirt than shorts that ride up your butt all the time," she says. "How am I supposed to run my fastest with a wedgie slowing me down?"

Raina snorts.

"If only we were shaped like boys," Chrissy says.

"If only we had uniforms for girls," I say.

"Are you ladies gonna stand out here moaning about if-onlys, or are you gonna get on the bus?" Coach Mac says.

We dutifully climb up the steps. When we collapse into our seats—Chrissy and Raina in one, me in another—Raina says, "If only Coach Mac could talk to the people in charge the way she talks to us."

"I think she probably does," I say. "But she's still a woman."

"Bossy," Chrissy says.

"Aggressive," Raina says.

"One of those feminists," I say, wrinkling my nose.

We laugh, but it's really not the kind of thing you laugh about for long—all those words they use to dismiss strong and fierce women. The sad and awful truth about the injustice of the world is never something we laugh about for long. Hardly at all, really. We're young, but we already know that.

Instead the three of us sit in silence and think. Or at least I do. And what I think is *But what about the sisterhood? Would they get people to listen?*

My nerves start jangling when we have about fifteen minutes left before we get to the track in Bloomington.

I'm not alone. The whole bus goes completely quiet.

It's weird. This isn't even district.

But maybe it's because of Natalie. We've all been running meets together all season, but now there's someone new in our group. No one knows what to expect from her.

I glance back at where I saw her sitting earlier. She's alone in the last seat. She stares out the window, watching the fields pass.

No one's even talked to her since she got on the bus. And I don't know if I feel sorry or satisfied that she's still an outcast.

So much for the sisterhood.

Pop has a seat in the stands right up front, so when I pass him on my way to line up for my heat, he shouts, "Run hard, Leta Lightning Laurel!"

He's wearing fluorescent orange short shorts I don't remember him having on this morning.

A couple of girls racing me snort and snicker.

They won't be laughing when I beat them.

I take off hard. Fast.

I fly.

I barely even notice the pain in my foot. I just run, one curve, one straightaway, one curve, last straightaway, home.

I'm first in the heat, which means I make it to finals.

Natalie does too.

My hands shake when we line up for the finals. I've never raced Natalie before. I should have. At least then I would know what to expect and where we stand.

We both take off hard. Fast.

We both fly.

Pain slices through my foot, but I tell myself it'll be over in less than a minute.

I run so hard my lungs feel like they might explode.

Natalie keeps pace with me.

But just when I think she might pull ahead, just when the pain in my foot moves from a yell to a scream, she drops behind. Gassed out.

I cross the finish line first.

I win.

I can hardly see for the white flashes that sneak across my vision in time with my heartbeat.

Coach Mac holds me up. Her voice comes to me from a long way off.

"Leta? What's wrong?"

The world starts to go black.

The last thing I hear is "Medic! Get the medic!"

Twenty-eight

SATURDAY

I'm not out long. It was probably just my body's response to the pain, taking me away for a merciful minute.

The medic hasn't reached me when the world comes back.

Pop has, though. His face moves over mine. He looks worried.

"You okay, Leta?"

I don't have time to answer before the medic pushes everyone away. But when I say "Pop!" he moves back beside me. I clutch his hand.

Coach Mac squats on the grass on my other side. "Jeez, Leta, when I told you to give it your all, I didn't mean kill yourself."

I manage a weak smile. The medic has my foot in his hands. He presses a tender spot, and I yell.

He looks at Coach Mac when he says, "Might be a stress fracture. We won't know without imaging."

"How long will that take to heal?" I say. I'm thinking a few days.

"Dammit," Coach Mac says.

When I look at Pop, his eyes don't meet mine.

That tells me just about everything I need to know.

Still, I say, "What does that mean?"

Coach Mac runs a hand over her mouth. "It means your season's over," she says.

No. That can't be it. I have to run in the district meet. I have to win it. I have to remind Dad he has a responsibility to take care of us. To be home with us.

I blink away the tears.

I can run through the pain. I will.

For Amelia.

Coach Mac won't let me run the mile relay, and I don't have it in me to argue.

The medic had a boot. He showed me how to put it on, strap everything, inflate the little balloon-like things on the sides to make it fit better. "If it's a fracture, you'll need crutches," he says. "You won't know without an X-ray or MRI."

I know Mom can't afford an X-ray or MRI, but I nod anyway. I'll just wear the boot, tell Mom it's a little sprain, nothing more.

I'll make sure Pop does the same.

Sabrina's the alternate for the mile relay, so she gets to run it. Natalie runs in my slot instead of the starting position. That makes me feel a little sick to my stomach. But I watch them anyway. I cheer them on anyway. They're my team.

Chrissy starts strong, hands off to Sabrina, who slows them down a little. But things get messy during Sabrina's handoff to Raina. Maybe Raina starts too fast, or maybe Sabrina's tired. They almost don't hand off in the designated arrows, but Raina stops completely and takes the baton. She works hard to catch up, and she passes a couple of people, but the lead runner is too far ahead. Not even Natalie will be able to catch her. She tries hard, but she comes in second.

I know it's wrong, but I can't help feeling a teeny bit glad they didn't win.

Maybe with me they would have.

I have to go to the bathroom. Pop helps me to the concrete building.

I don't realize Natalie followed us until she says, "I can help her inside."

She's shorter than me by at least four inches, but she's strong. I put an arm over her shoulder and lean into her, trying not to put too much weight on my booted foot.

I'm glad to see that as bad as this day has been, I haven't had a surprise visit from my period. Coach Mac showed us all how to count twenty-eight days from the first day of our periods to try to predict when the next one would come. But she warned us that not all cycles were predictable, especially in the beginning. Mine sort of is, but sometimes it comes on day twenty-seven and sometimes it waits until day thirty-one. I think I'm close to day twenty-seven.

Natalie doesn't say anything until I'm washing my hands.

"I had one of those before," she says.

"What?"

"You know. A stress fracture."

I drop my eyes to the sink, where soap bubbles gather on the silver drain. I try to tell her it's not a stress fracture, but the words get stuck.

"I was out six weeks," Natalie says. The words hang around us, pulsing like one of the lights in the corner. "I came back stronger."

But she doesn't understand. I don't want to leave.

And I don't have six weeks.

Natalie walks with me and Pop back to the tent.

The meet's not over, but I just want to go home. I'm sure Coach Mac will let me.

Pop says, "That was some fantastic running you did out there, Natalie."

My chest squeezes, and I hate myself for it. If we're a sisterhood, why am I jealous?

When I look at Natalie, her smile is so sad I have to look right back away. And my chest squeezes even more. Because I think she knows.

"Thanks," she says, so softly you could pretend it was the wind.

We watch her walk away, looking like she carries something heavy on her shoulders.

Pop hugs me tight. And I don't deserve it at all.

Pop's quiet on the car ride home. Coach Mac let me skip the bus. Raina and Chrissy hugged me tight before waving me out of the parking lot.

I keep trying to figure out how to convince Pop not to

say anything to Mom about what happened today.

Finally, he breaks the ice. "So?" he says. "How are you feeling?"

I shrug. "Okay."

"Really?" he says. He sounds like he doesn't believe me. He can see right through me.

I shrug.

"We won't know anything without an X-ray," he says. "And sometimes stress fractures don't even show up on that. You have to get an MRI."

All those things just sound more and more expensive.

"You know Mom can't afford all that." I say the words so quietly I'm not sure if he can hear them. It's a whisper of a whisper.

Pop doesn't say anything. I let the silence wrap around us for a while before I say, "What if we didn't tell Mom?"

I feel Pop's eyes on me for a second, but I don't meet them. "You mean . . ." He lets the words trail off.

"I mean tell her I have a sprain. Nothing serious." Now I look at Pop. He glances at me every now and then, in between looking at the road like a responsible driver. "You know, so she doesn't worry."

"You mean so you can keep running," Pop says.

I don't answer that. He knows me. How could I lie?

"It's not good to run on a stress fracture," he says. "You

could turn it into something more serious. An actual fracture that takes you out for years."

"We don't even know if that's what it is," I say.

"But whatever's going on with your foot, your body's telling you it needs rest."

"My body's strong," I say. "It can handle this."

Pop shakes his head, teeth worrying his lower lip. But he doesn't argue.

And that feels like a win.

After more minutes of a silence that feels thick and loaded with all the things we aren't saying, Pop says, "I've had a stress fracture before. Back when I was younger and pushed myself too hard."

"You did?" I can't imagine Pop taking any time off running. If he doesn't get to run, he gets really grumpy and no one wants to be around him.

"Didn't stop me, either."

See? I knew it.

"I didn't run on it, though."

"What?" My heart sinks.

"I went to the pool," Pop says. "Maintained my fitness."

"I'm not a swimmer," I say. I don't mention that I can't imagine how swimming is anything like running.

"I didn't swim," Pop says. "I did some pool running."

"Pool running? What's that?"

Pop grins at me. "You run in a pool."

He's making this up. He has to be. I'm probably looking at him like I think he's gone off the deep end.

"In the deep end," he says, like he can read my mind. "With a special floating belt."

"That sounds about as fun as running on a treadmill," I say.

Pop shrugs. "Or round and round a track."

I guess a track could get pretty boring if you're running twenty miles.

"I'll talk to your coach," Pop says. He seems to be talking mostly to himself. "See if she'll let me train you. I'll make sure you can run by district."

I guess he forgot district's next week.

But I don't remind him. I just say, "Promise?"

And he says, "Promise."

Pop doesn't break promises anymore.

When Mom asks how the meet went, all Pop says is "She took first place."

But then she wants to know all about the boot on my

foot, why I'm wearing it, what she needs to do to follow up and make sure everything's okay.

All I say is "It's just a little sprain."

Mom cocks her head at me. "It's been bothering you for a while. I've seen you limping." She looks from me to Pop and back again. "Did something happen at the meet to make it worse?"

"Nothing we can't handle with a little rehab," Pop says.

Mom narrows her eyes, trying to see through Pop's assurances. But Pop doesn't waver. And when she looks at me I say, "I'll be fine," and hope she doesn't say anything about district next week.

She doesn't.

After a while, Pop leaves us to our supper. When he hugs me good-bye, he says, "I'll steal you from practice on Monday. Be ready with your swimsuit."

Ugh. Running in my swimsuit. I'll just wear a shirt and shorts. Swimsuits make me uncomfortable. I think about all those professional runners who have to wear the short shorts and the tops that look like sports bras. How does anyone get comfortable putting their bodies on display like that? Because I may only be thirteen, but I already know a girl's body is always on display. It's why the girls at school talk the way they do. And why the boys have their lists.

I kiss Pop on the cheek.

He'll fix everything.

I just know it.

"Where's Amelia?" I say after Pop's left and it's just me and Mom.

"Eating supper with her friends." She gestures to the house at the end of the driveway behind us.

I remember I never talked to Mom about Amelia going to that house when she was home alone. I don't want to be a snitch, but I tell Mom anyway.

Mom shakes her head. "That girl," she says, then sighs. "I guess I'll have to ask Pop to come over, make sure she doesn't break the rules again."

Her eyes look so tired.

Sometimes you think you're doing what's right, telling your mom a truth your sister won't tell, but all you really do is add to her burden. I should have just kept quiet, dealt with it myself.

But like Pop always says, the truth is much clearer to see when you're looking back at it.

Twenty-nine

SUNDAY

My letter project is due in two weeks. I can't seem to write any other letter until I've written Dad's. So I might be doomed.

I try to work on it again tonight, but I don't get anywhere. Just a bunch of crossed-out *Dear Dad*s.

How do you know where to start when there's so much to say?

Amelia dominates the chair today.

She sits there for hours, getting up only once to go to the bathroom at the same time I head into the kitchen for a snack. And by the time I realize she's left the chair empty, she vaults out the bathroom door and lands in the chair, a victorious look on her face.

This boot makes me slow, and she knows it. (Which also doesn't make her victorious, by the way. It makes her taking advantage of an unfair situation.)

Time for another strategy. Time to dial up the torture. Time to win.

Round 4

I open the can of Spam, fan its disgusting aroma toward the living room. I really have no idea why Mom still buys this stuff. It's cheap, I guess.

Amelia sits up straight in the chair and locks eyes with me.

I slide a small sliver out and spoon it into my mouth and manage (I hope) to make it look like it's the most delicious thing I've ever tasted.

Amelia crawls to the edge of the chair. It tips, but she catches herself and slides back to the seat.

"Funny," I say. "Mom just got groceries, but . . ." I shrug. "This is the last can of Spam."

This stuff is disgusting, but you'd be surprised the kind of sacrifices you're willing to make for a comfy chair like that one. I could put up my foot and maybe it would stop throbbing for a little while.

Amelia makes a noise, halfway between a choke and a whimper. I have her right where I want her.

I slide another chunk of Spam into my mouth and down my throat. I have to work *very* hard not to let it come back up.

"That's mine!" Amelia yells. "You know it is!"

"Says who?" I say.

"You don't even like it!"

"Says who?"

Amelia folds her arms across her chest.

"There's still a lot left in this can," I say. I try not to wrinkle my nose while I say it. I wedge another piece onto my spoon and shove it into my mouth. If I have to do this for much longer, I'm going to vomit. "But it's going fast."

I move toward the table, set down the can, and pretend to turn away, maybe for some water, maybe for some of Amelia's favorite crackers, which she likes to eat with Spam.

I hear the chair whine behind me. I smile. So predictable.

Amelia's fast, but this time I'm faster. I leap into the chair, beating Amelia by a split second. We're so close she sloshes some Spam juice out of the can and onto my boot.

Gross.

Amelia glares at me. "You don't even like Spam."

I shrug. "So? I needed to put my foot up, and you've been hogging the chair all day."

She's mad, but she'll be even madder when she sees the other two cans of Spam in the pantry.

You do all sorts of things you're not proud of when it comes to this chair.

Amelia huffs away, taking the smell of Spam with her.

I can't say I'm not glad.

Thirty

MONDAY

Mrs. Crisp doesn't ask about our projects. She just sets us loose to work on them during class and stays mostly at her desk.

I stare at a blank page for practically the entire period, with the exception of trying a few other names. *Dear Mom. Dear Sabrina. Dear younger Leta.* I cross them all out.

If I don't have any ideas by Friday, I guess I'll be writing my letters to some imaginary people. I know Mrs. Crisp said we could only do that for one category, but she doesn't have to know they're imaginary Amelias and imaginary Sabrinas and imaginary Moms and Dads. Or imaginary people entirely. I can make up someone I love and someone I admire and someone I'd like to know better and someone who hurt me and someone who meant a lot to me once but isn't around anymore.

Imagination is sometimes easier than reality.

Pop shows up at my practice just as the group has finished the warm-up lap.

I help Natalie with her stretches, but I don't run a single step. I haven't taken off the boot since Saturday. Except to shower. Of course I've showered. And I washed the Spam splashes off it so Coach Mac wouldn't start complaining about how bad my boot smells too.

I watch Pop talk to Coach Mac. When he moves toward the high jump patch, I hear someone say, "Here comes the weird old man in short shorts."

Briana. I give her my fiercest glare, my face bursting into flames.

Pop stops beside Natalie and me. "All right, Lagging Leta." I don't like that nickname very much. "Coach says you're all mine."

Someone giggles. Probably Briana. I glare at her again, and this time I don't miss the smile on Sabrina's face.

I really don't like mean girls. And I don't understand why they're still being this way after Coach Mac's talk last week. Most of the other girls get it. I've heard a couple of them tell Ryan he can't say things like "You run like a girl" to Quentin. Because girls are fast and strong, and it's not an insult to be one.

I'm gonna have to talk to Pop about his silly nicknames too.

"Where are you going?" Natalie says.

"To the pool," Pop says, gesturing toward the direction of the town's public pool, which happens to be right across the street. "For some pool running."

Someone else snorts, but I don't bother to see who. I follow Pop toward the parking lot.

When I glance back, Natalie's staring at us like she wishes she could join us.

Pop doesn't get in the pool with me. He says he needs to watch the clock so he can tell me when to pick it up and when to rest.

I don't know what we're doing or how to do this. I've never even liked pools.

Pop hands me a belt. "Put the bulky part on your back," he says. "Snap it in the front."

"What's this?"

"A pool running belt. The kind professionals use." He wiggles his eyebrows like that's supposed to mean something. And I guess it does. It means professional runners use pool running to keep in shape. Which means this might work.

I snap the belt in place.

"Now take off your boot and get in," Pop says.

The water's cold. Pop waves me toward the deep end, where my feet can't touch bottom, which honestly makes me a little nervous. I remind myself I have a floating belt. I'm not gonna drown.

Pop holds up his phone like it's a stopwatch. "Ready?" he says.

"I don't even know what I'm doing," I say.

"You're running," Pop says.

"In the water?"

"Exactly," Pop says. "Now go!"

It's a lot harder than it sounds.

My arms and legs don't move the same way in water as they do on land. Pop says to watch my form, bring the knees up, arc the legs forward, kick them back.

"Almost like riding an imaginary bicycle," Pop says.

I just try to run.

Before five minutes I'm breathless.

"That's just the warm-up," Pop says. He grins. "Now you'll sprint a four hundred."

He makes me close my eyes and calls out every curve and straightaway. He tells me to picture it in my mind.

We do this twenty-four times.

Pop finally says, "Okay, that's enough for the day."

I can hardly breathe. But my legs and feet feel fresh. And my foot didn't scream once.

Maybe Pop knows what he's doing.

I feel like I could eat an entire restaurant after all that pool running. Pop says it's because my body had to work extra hard on the running and on regulating my temperature in the water.

"Where'd you learn about pool running?" I ask him when we're halfway home.

He shrugs. "Every serious runner knows about it. Most runners get injured at some point in their career and have to figure out something else to do to hang on to their fitness."

"You could bike," I say. I know this will get him riled.

Pop splutters. "Bike? Runners don't bike, Lightning." And he launches off about how much better running is than biking. His best friend is a long-distance biker. They have debates about this for fun. For hours.

I can hardly keep from laughing. I guess Pop notices, because he stops and gives me a side-eye. "I see what you did," he says. He laughs too. "Good to see you smiling again."

What's he mean by that?

Maybe he hears the question in my silence. He says, "You're so serious all the time, Leta. Taking care of Amelia, doing your schoolwork, running to win. Don't you ever have fun?"

"Running's fun," I say.

"Is it?" Pop stares at the road. My cheeks start to burn. "Running *should* be fun," he says. "But it's not fun to always feel pressured to win."

He doesn't understand. Besides, how does a person become the best without winning?

Pop's not finished, and we still have seven miles to go before we get home.

"There's nothing wrong with wanting to win, Leta," he says. "But if winning is your life, the reason you do something well, you have to keep winning. And if you aren't enough without winning, you'll never be enough, no matter how many gold medals you bring home."

I pretend I don't know what he's talking about, but my heart tells a different story. It pounds and pounds and pounds. It says, *Never enough. Never enough. Never enough.*

Pop squeezes my hand. "You're the most remarkable

thirteen-year-old I've ever met." The next words he says so softly I tell myself I only imagine them. "I sure wish you could believe that."

Mom is sitting at the table when Pop drops me home. I let the screen door slam behind me. She winces, so I say, "Sorry." I always forget to catch the screen door before it slams. The wood is starting to split. I really should remember.

Mom smiles at me. "How was practice?"

"Good." I swallow hard.

"You did some pool running, Pop said."

"Yeah." I have to be careful. If Mom finds out what's *really* going on with my foot, she'll take me straight to the ER for an X-ray. And we don't have the money for that.

I know, because after she went to bed last night, I snuck back to the table and pulled her checkbook out of her purse so I could look at it. I wasn't being nosy. I just wanted to know. She doesn't talk to us about money, and sometimes the not-talking makes it worse.

We have seventy dollars left until the next time she gets paid, which is a little less than two weeks away. And we're still behind on practically everything.

She'd tell me I shouldn't worry about that. But how can I not? What if we have to move out? Where would we live?

Pop's house isn't big enough for the three of us.

"Why pool running?" Mom says, tearing me out of my near-panic train of thought. "The big meet's this weekend, isn't it?"

She knows it is. She has it marked on her calendar, circled in red. She already took the day off.

"Coach Mac wants me to rest my joints," I say. A half-truth. "Pool running is the closest thing you'll get to running without the impact." I'm just repeating what Pop told me.

"Hmm." I can't tell if Mom stopped listening or if she's just thinking. After a second she says, "Your supper's in the microwave."

It's a big glob of gummy Hamburger Helper.

I'm tired of Hamburger Helper.

I eat half of it, put the other half in the container with the rest of the leftovers, and try to convince myself I'm not hungry enough to eat a restaurant.

Lighter sometimes is faster, I tell myself. *I'll only do it until the district meet.*

It's easier to do what you know is wrong (because your coach is constantly talking about how wrong it is) when you tell yourself it's not forever.

Thirty-one

TUESDAY

I wake up to the presence of my period.

I was expecting it, kind of, but you never really expect it. No matter how many periods you have, there's still this heart-lurch that happens when you see blood, either on your underwear or on the toilet paper. It's like a tiny little moment of *Oh god, I'm dying*. And then you remember. You have a period. This blood is normal.

I know I should be used to it. Maybe even glad for it. But it's really just an achy inconvenience, you know?

Mom stocks the cabinet under the sink with tampons and pads of all sizes—with wings because she says everybody needs wings. I haven't been brave enough to try the tampons yet, so I grab a few pads I can stuff in my backpack.

I know by now to hide them well, because some people—boys and girls—act like it's the grossest thing to see pads sticking out of pockets. Even though it's perfectly natural. Every day someone at the junior high is probably on their period. Why do we act like it's such a shameful thing? Because it's associated with girls, who are inferior to boys? It's stupid.

Sometimes society wins when it shouldn't.

I guess that's why we need a sisterhood. I think of Coach Mac's words. *Nothing can stand against a sisterhood.*

I leave my pads sticking out of my backpack pockets. No one gets to make me feel ashamed.

Just before I leave the house, I remember: I'm getting in a pool today. Which is not a problem most days. Except that today I'm on my period.

How do you manage your period when you have to "run" in a pool? I don't think I can wear a pad. Is that what tampons are for?

Mom talked about all this with me, way back in the beginning, but I don't remember everything. I think I was too busy being embarrassed, which I know is stupid but which is also a little uncontrollable. Did she mention tampons?

I open the cabinet under the sink again. A box of tampons hides behind the collection of pads.

My stomach feels all squishy. I stare at the tampon box for a long time before I bend down and take one out. I have no idea how to use them, and Mom's already gone for the day.

Being a girl is hard. No one teaches you about this stuff, you know? Boys get to learn all kinds of things about their changing bodies, but no one tells the girls, "This is how you use a tampon, if you choose to."

I grab a few more from the package and hope for the best.

In English class Mrs. Crisp says, "How's everyone's letter project coming along?" Her eyes sweep the room, resting on me.

I knew I couldn't hide forever. I pretend my shoe's untied and dip my head under the desk.

I haven't even started my project.

Eight letters due next Friday. One to each person in each category, four to one of them. Will I have time to work on them this weekend? I doubt it. I'm running out of time. I try to ignore the panic. I have to make good grades. I know that. But I just can't make myself get started on the letter project.

I'll do them tonight. All eight letters. I have to. You

can't perfect letters that don't even exist yet. And I need the weekend to perfect them. I've never procrastinated this long on a project.

My throat gets so tight I feel like I might stop breathing.

Mrs. Crisp says, "Anyone want to share one of their letters?"

No one says a word.

And because no one says a word, I know what's coming even before Mrs. Crisp says, "Leta? How about you?"

I'm usually the student who answers every question, volunteers to share, and has all the definitions to the literary techniques we talk about.

I've never not shared before. Will Mrs. Crisp be disappointed if I say no, in front of everyone?

The silence around us gets heavier and heavier, eyes burning my back and neck and cheeks, until I say, "Mine's kind of private?"

A question, like I'm asking permission to say the words. To keep my letters private, even though Mrs. Crisp said, back in the beginning, that we wouldn't have to share if we didn't want to.

Mrs. Crisp says, "I understand, Leta. Anyone else?"

Every other person she calls on says the exact same thing. I can't tell if they're making fun of me or trying to get out of sharing too.

It doesn't matter. After what feels like a lifetime, the bell rings, and we're free.

I'm not free, though. Before I slide out the door, Mrs. Crisp says, "Leta? Can I see you for a minute?"

I have lunch now, so I don't have anywhere I really need to be. I didn't bring a lunch today, and I didn't ask Chrissy to bring me any of her mom's cooking. I haven't asked her to bring me anything in . . . well, I stopped counting how many days.

I wonder if Mrs. Crisp is mad at me for not sharing. For providing the example that every other classmate used to get out of sharing.

She waits until the room has cleared to say, "I haven't checked in with you lately. I just wondered how everything is going."

Does she check in with all her students? And if not, why just me? Am I the kind of student who needs extra help? Am I the kind of student teachers feel sorry for, because of where I come from?

The questions heat up my face. I glance toward the door. "Everything's fine," I say. I try to make it sound true.

Mrs. Crisp says, "I noticed you're wearing a boot."

I shrug. "Just a little sprain. From running, you know."

Mrs. Crisp smiles now. "I've heard about how fast you are on a track."

What?

"You're kind of legendary among the sixth graders."

I forgot Mrs. Crisp's daughter is a sixth grader who wants to run track. We talked to the sixth-grade athletics class at the beginning of the season, and Maren Crisp was one of the girls who raised her hand and blurted out, "I want to run the four hundred."

Mrs. Crisp's words should make me feel warm. Dad would come home for a legend, wouldn't he? If that's actually what I was?

But instead her words make me feel heavy, and it's not just my foot hurting me now. My throat hurts and my chest hurts and my whole stupid body hurts.

Mrs. Crisp waves a hand and says, "Okay, go on to lunch. But let me know if you need anything. Anything at all."

I limp out the door on my boot. No sense pretending anymore that I'm not injured in the places you can see.

It's better than people knowing how injured I am in the places you can't see.

When I finally make it to the picnic table under the tree, Chrissy and Raina look at me with the kinds of expressions that say *I'm so, so sorry I have to tell you this.*

My throat closes up again. More bad news? The universe is really trying hard today.

"What?" I say in a strangled-sounding voice. Did I leak? Am I walking around with bloodstains on the back of my pants? I just changed my pad an hour ago, and it wasn't that bad.

Chrissy and Raina look at each other and share something that leaves me out. If Sabrina were here, we might do the same, the two of us. But she's all the way across the grass, eating with Briana and Brooke and all the other cheerleaders. She doesn't even look my way.

Raina says, "You tell her."

Chrissy shakes her head. "You."

"Tell me what?" Fear singes my words, and anger, too. Maybe I should have hidden those pads instead of letting the whole world see them. Is that what this is about?

I guess everyone *does* get to make me feel ashamed. It's so confusing. Sometimes I feel so strong and other times I feel so weak. Why do we have to deal with all this extra crap just because we're girls?

"We'll tell her together," Raina says. Chrissy nods. They take a deep breath and say, "They made another list," in the exact same way, almost like they practiced it.

At first I don't know what they're talking about.

Raina says. "You know, Girls with the Hairiest Legs? Girls from the Poorest Families?"

I didn't even know she knew about those lists. I never told her. But of course she knew. She was on two of them.

My legs turn to mush, like I've just run fifty four hundreds.

Which list did I make this time?

I almost don't want to ask the question, but I swallow hard and say, "What was the list?"

"Well, there were a few," Raina says. "We had some extra time in science, and some people used it to . . ."

"Put girls on lists?" I say.

Raina nods. "The worst ones were Girls Who Are Losers and Girls with the Worst Clothes." She stares at the picnic table.

I sit. "And I guess I'm on them." It's not a question.

Raina and Chrissy look at each other. They're not telling me something.

"You were only on one of them at first," Chrissy says.

"Girls Who Are Losers," I say. It's just a guess. My clothes are fine . . . I think. But I could see a boy thinking it would be funny to put me on a loser list now that I'm walking around in a boot.

Chrissy nods.

"But then you were added to the second one," Raina says.

"Sabrina added your name," Chrissy says.

Sabrina?

You don't think you can possibly break any more—and just like that, you do.

"It was probably a joke," Chrissy says.

"She probably didn't mean for people to see it," Raina says.

Does that matter?

"It doesn't matter," I say, answering my own silent question. My mouth is so dry you'd think I ran the entire 1.6-mile course Coach Mac makes us run every Monday in athletics class without a bit of water waiting at the end—and then ran it six more times.

She shouldn't have put me on any stupid, embarrassing list, even if it was a joke. Even if she didn't mean for people to see it. That's not what best friends are supposed to do. It's not what sisterhoods do.

I don't understand what happened, why she started hanging out with those other girls. Why she left behind a friendship of eight years. A good friendship. A great one.

Before I can turn around and glare in her direction, someone says, "There's nothing wrong with the way you dress. Those kids are stupid. And petty."

Natalie Dash.

She pauses only long enough to meet my eyes, and then she moves on to a shady spot beside the school building, leaning her head back against the faded brick.

None of us join her.

The last thing Raina says about the lists is "Benny Dunlap tore them up."

Even that doesn't make me feel warm inside.

My foot starts throbbing. I prop it on the bench, where Sabrina used to sit every day.

I tell it, *We'll show them.*

We'll show them all.

Thirty-two

TUESDAY

I wear pads all day until right after school. I tell Chrissy and Raina, "Tell Coach Mac to wait for me. I need to go to the bathroom."

Our junior high doesn't have a track, so Coach Mac has to drive us to the high school track every day for practice. Hopefully she won't leave without me. And hopefully this won't take too long.

I close myself in a stall. I unzip my backpack and take out one of the tampons. I open the package. I don't know what to do from there.

The door squeals, and someone comes into the bathroom.

"Leta?"

It's Raina.

"You okay?"

"Yeah, everything's fine," I say. My voice sounds strained and not even a little bit fine.

"You sure?" Raina says. "It's just . . . your face."

What's wrong with my face?

"You looked like . . ." Raina pauses. "Like you swallowed a handful of candy corn and were about to throw up again."

That happened at Halloween last year. I don't like candy corn. And someone dared me to eat a handful. It did not end well for either of us.

I groan. "I'm on my period," I say.

"Oh yeah." Understanding slides through those two words.

The door squeals open again. "Leta? Raina?"

It's Chrissy this time.

"I thought I told y'all to let Coach Mac know I was in the bathroom!" I say. If no one tells her, she'll leave us all! Coach Mac does not wait for anyone or anything.

"I did," Chrissy says. "But . . . your face."

"I know," I say.

"She's on her period," Raina says.

"Oh yeah." The same understanding slides through Chrissy's two words.

"I just need to . . ." I trail off. It's a little embarrassing saying it out loud. I don't know why. We're kind of taught not to talk about periods (except from Coach Mac, but who is one person or even a handful of people against an entire society?). And we especially don't talk about the period supplies you need to use.

Maybe it's time to change that.

"Have you ever used a tampon?" I say.

"That's all I use," Raina says. "They're so much more convenient."

"I've used them a few times," Chrissy says. "Especially during the summer. You know, swimming all the time. Can't let your period stop you from swimming!"

They sound like commercials.

"You're not getting paid to advertise tampons," I say.

"Have you ever used a tampon?" Chrissy says.

"No," I say. "But I need to."

I let the words hang there, thinking they'll get what I'm asking. But neither of them offers any information, so I have to come out and say it.

"How do you, you know . . . ?"

"Put it in?" Raina says.

"Yeah."

"You just slide it in," Chrissy says.

"Well, it depends on the kind you have," Raina says. "You want to let us in?"

"NO!" I know we're supposed to be a sisterhood, but I'm not ready to let them in the stall and watch me put a tampon in.

Someone snorts. It's probably Chrissy. And that's confirmed when Chrissy says, "You're so weird, Raina. Who wants someone watching them put in a tampon?"

"My grandma taught me how to use them," Raina says. "It was really helpful. It's just anatomy, you know."

"How about I describe it to you?" I say.

"We'll see if that works," Raina says. She sounds doubtful.

This is taking much longer than I thought.

"It's long," I say. "It looks like there's a bottom tube and another tube that goes into it?"

"Okay," Raina says. "That's the kind I use. So you'll want to stick the bigger part, the one without the string hanging out, in your vagina—"

"Raina!" Chrissy says.

"Oh, please," Raina says. "It's just anatomy. Vagina's the name for it."

My face gets hotter and hotter, even though I'm with my best friends. Even though I'm with girls who deal with their periods on a monthly basis. Even though everybody currently in this bathroom has a vagina.

Why am I embarrassed? It's annoying.

"Okay," I say. "Should I stand or sit or what?"

"It's really whatever makes you most comfortable," Raina says.

"I usually stand and squat a little," Chrissy says. "Like, a mini squat."

I try that. "What next?" I say.

"So you'll want to hold the tampon in the center of the stick," Raina says. "Right where the fatter tube and the thinner tube meet. And then you'll push it up your vagina until your fingers are touching your labia."

"What's the labia?" I say. I thought Mom had explained everything, but clearly Raina's had a better education. Her grandma's a nurse, so I guess that makes sense.

"The folds of skin around your vulva," Raina says.

"I thought we were talking about a vagina," I say.

"We are," Raina says. "It's all part of the vagina. I mean, sort of. I'll show you a drawing if you really need it."

"Nope. Let's just get this over with before Coach Mac leaves all three of us here," I say.

"So as soon as you have enough of the bigger part of the stick in your vagina"—seriously, how many times is she going to say the word?—"then you push the smaller part into the bigger part, and that's what releases the tampon and protects you from bleeding all over the place."

I do what she says. "There's still a stick hanging out of me," I say. "It's very uncomfortable."

"Oh," Raina says. "That's just the applicator. You can take that out and throw it away."

I take it out and throw it away.

"You should have a string hanging out now," Raina says.

"Yeah," I say.

"When you're ready to change your tampon, you just pull the string," Raina says. "And it'll come out."

"Okay."

"And it shouldn't be painful or anything," Raina says. "You should forget it's even there."

"It doesn't feel painful."

"That means it's in right!" Raina says. She sounds excited, like I've just done something remarkable, even though millions probably do this every day.

"You'll need to change it every four hours or so," Chrissy says. "Don't leave it in too long. It's dangerous."

"But we don't need to get into the specifics of why it's dangerous," Raina says. I imagine her eyeing Chrissy with a *You know she has anxiety* look. "Just remember to change it every four hours."

Four hours gives me enough time to do my workout and get home. I'll just take it out as soon as I get home.

And that's how I learn to use a tampon.

I hope every girl has the kind of friends who can teach them how to use a tampon.

Pop takes me to the pool again. This time he tells me to sprint for a minute and a half, rest thirty seconds.

"But I run a four hundred faster than a minute and a half," I say.

"I know you do. But we shoot higher, and you do even better in the shorter sprints."

I sure hope he's right.

By the fifth interval, I'm breathing harder than I would be if I'd run on the track. There's something about all that water, pressing on my legs and arms, that makes me feel like I'm running my first race ever, without months of conditioning behind me.

Am I even in shape?

Maybe it's the not-eating. Maybe I should float an innocent question to Pop on the way home. Something like "What should I be eating to make sure I have the most power for my race?" I'm not completely convinced lighter isn't faster, but it's good to have a backup plan.

"You sure this is going to work?" I huff after the tenth interval. I'm counting. Pop says I have to do thirty today. Twenty more feels like torture.

Pop shrugs. "I know Olympians use the pool at the first twinge of injury."

If it's good enough for Olympians, I guess it's good enough for me.

I just hope I remember how to run on land when I get there again.

Once the pool running practice is over, I feel like I could sleep on the concrete that lines the pool. I don't know if I can even walk to the car.

I'm so hungry, my stomach feels queasy. Pop hands me a package of snack mix. I dig in.

Pop says, "Good work, Leta."

I stretch my foot and feel it pinch. I put my boot back on but decide today's the day when I'll stop wearing it at home. Mom needs to know I can walk without a boot before she'll let me run in the meet on Saturday. I'll stuff it in my backpack and only use it where she can't see.

I tell myself a little pain never hurt anybody.

I ask Pop my innocent food question. He talks most of the way home about the best food for runners—nuts, avocados (Mom doesn't buy those), olive oil, any kind of vegetable, whole-grain breads and pastas. He goes on and on and on. Half those foods are too expensive for Mom to buy.

So I say, "What if you're on a budget?"

Pop glances at me and back at the road. "You can't go wrong with beans and rice," he says. "Perfect protein. And super cheap."

Beans and rice. I can handle that. I'll ask Mom to get some.

"Just make sure you're eating enough," Pop says. "When runners don't get enough nutrition, they get injured more easily."

Oh. My heart speeds up.

"And it makes those injuries last a lot longer."

Well, I guess he's convinced me. "Lighter is faster" *is* a myth, like Coach Mac said. Lighter is just more dangerous. At least when you stop eating to be lighter.

I stare out the window and try to reconcile that with all the messages we constantly get from the world about how skinny we should be. Regular girls, of course, all the time and everywhere, but also girl *athletes*. Runners. Most of the female runners I've seen look like they're nothing but skin, bone, and muscle. It's so confusing.

We're quiet until Pop turns on the road home. That's when I say, "Thank you for not telling Mom about my foot." I start unstrapping the boot.

Pop doesn't say anything. When I look at him, he bites his lip like he has something to say but doesn't quite know how to do it.

"What?" I say.

Pop glances at me, then back at the road. "I know how important this meet is to you, Leta." He glances at me again. "I just want to make sure you run it for you, not anyone else."

I keep my face frozen, don't give anything away. I just say, "I run it for me."

Pop nods and offers a small smile. He says, "Okay." And again, softer: "Okay."

I can't tell if he believes me.

The tampon comes out when I pull the string, just like Raina said it would. It's a little uncomfortable, and you don't want to know what it looks like.

I wrap it in toilet paper, bury it in the trash, and we never have to speak of it again.

Thirty-three

TUESDAY

I try again to write a letter to Dad, but every time I think of something to say, I talk myself out of it. It's not even a conscious decision. I pick up my pen, try to write words, and only end up with scribbles.

"Are you trying to draw?" Amelia says. I didn't even know she'd come into the room. I try to hide the page before I ball it up and throw it in the trash can, where it belongs.

"No." She knows me better than that. I don't draw.

"Good," Amelia says. "'Cause that didn't look like anything."

Not a letter, either. I'm glad.

I don't know why the words feel so hard to find. How many times have I imagined what I'd say to Dad if I saw him again?

I guess they're just not things I want to put down on paper.

I take out a fresh sheet. If I can just get started on the others, I'll feel like I'm making progress. I stare at the list. Someone I love, someone I admire, someone I'd like to know better, someone who hurt me, someone who meant a lot but isn't around anymore.

My brain feels like it's a field of fog.

Who? it whines. *Who?*

It sounds like an owl having a temper tantrum.

I write, *Dear Sabrina.*

And that's as far as I get because every time I think of Sabrina, I just see her with Brooke and Briana, laughing over those awful lists. Adding my name to another.

My face heats up to gas burner hot. My head fills with angry words, but I could never say them, especially not on paper for a school project. Because what if Mrs. Crisp told?

Besides, how do you write a letter to a best friend who betrayed you?

I know Raina probably wrote to Chrissy for one of the categories and Chrissy to Raina. Who does that leave me? Maybe I should write a letter to an imaginary friend I admire. I could invent a friend who lives far away, and no one would ever know. Mrs. Crisp didn't say we had to prove the people in our letters exist.

"I'm going to bed," Amelia says. What she's really saying is I should turn out the light.

So I give up for the night and try not to think about how time's running out.

For everything.

I thought I might be the last one up, but when I come out of the bathroom, the door sticking and opening with a loud crack, Mom's at the kitchen table. She looks up when I pass through. Her eyes look swollen, like maybe she's been crying. "Mom?"

"What's the matter, baby?"

It's what I should be asking her. I shake my head. "Nothing."

I move a little closer so I can see what she's working on. It's the checkbook, but I can't see the numbers.

Earlier today I heard Mom and Pop talking about money. Still none from Dad, just stretching things until payday. Same as always. Except prices are going higher, and Mom's salaries can't keep up.

My chest pinches.

Mom smiles at me, but it just makes her look sadder. "I didn't even get to ask you about practice today."

I shrug. "It was great."

Mom nods. "I'm so proud of you, Leta."

"For what?" I haven't done anything special. Haven't won anything that really matters.

Mom touches my cheek with her fingers. "You're just so . . . determined. You work so hard to get what you want."

I swallow a gigantic, prickly cactus arm. I already know enough about life to know that working hard doesn't mean you'll get what you want. Not for people like us.

If that were true, Mom would have Dad. She wouldn't worry about money, and she would only have to work one job—the one she loves.

Mom hugs me tight. "You inspire me," she says.

My throat hurts so bad I can't even tell her the same.

On the way to my room, I turn to look at her curved back, face hunched over that checkbook.

It takes a long time to fall asleep with an image like that burned into your mind.

See, I'm not just doing this for Amelia. I'm doing it for Mom, too.

I have to be enough for all of us.

"I have to be enough," I whisper into the universe.

Maybe my plea will convince someone or something out there to heal my foot so I can run.

Thirty-four

WEDNESDAY

I wake up remembering my period. It's a very loud reminder—backache, that weird sloshy feeling in my stomach, and also oozing I can't control, which is normal but never feels normal because it's uncontrollable.

Ugh.

I don't usually care so much. A period is a period. You deal with it. But I'm getting in a pool again today. Which means tampons. I'm still not super comfortable using them.

My sigh lasts a whole minute, I swear.

It would be so easy to be a boy.

I stop by the bathroom after school again. Raina and Chrissy already know to tell Coach Mac I'll be a little late.

But this time I get the tampon in much faster than I did yesterday.

Coach Mac always says, "Practice makes progress." Turns out it works for using period supplies too.

After another pool-running workout, Pop says, "I don't know if I've ever seen anyone run that long in the pool. How'd you manage to chase away your boredom?"

Pop had me run fifty four hundreds this time, so I was in the pool for more than ninety minutes. Pop brings his Bluetooth speaker so we can listen to Lizzo and Dua Lipa and Ava Max, but it's still hard not to get so bored your focus slips.

"It helps when you call out the curves and straights," I say.

I don't tell him I also thought about all the things I'd say to Dad after I win the district meet and Dad comes home apologizing for forgetting his kids.

Some things aren't worth mentioning out loud.

"And good music," Pop says.

Pop usually only listens to music from the '50s and '60s. Says they were the best eras for music.

"You like Lizzo now?" I say. "Lady Gaga? Beyoncé?"

Pop grins at me.

I follow him out to the car. "One more practice," he says. He glances back. "How's your foot feeling?"

The pain still needles a little, but it's not as bad as it was. So I say, "I think it's almost healed!"

Coach Mac said she wouldn't let me run in the meet if there's any pain whatsoever, but she doesn't have to know, does she? I've learned to hide emotional pain. I'm sure I can hide physical pain too.

"You don't want to mess anything up permanently, do you?" she said. "It's not worth giving up a high school career in track."

Running one race—two, if you count the relay—won't mess anything up permanently.

I feel Pop's eyes on me, but I pretend to rub something off my arm.

"Uh-huh," Pop says.

I imagine he's agreeing.

I'm not sure what exactly makes me say, "Hey, Pop? Why do you think Dad's not sending us any money?" when we're still ten minutes away from home.

Maybe the pool running demanded so much concentration and focus, I don't have enough left to keep quiet. And when a question's been bouncing around in your head for as long as this one has, it's nearly impossible not to let it slip.

Pop doesn't answer for a long time—so long, I start to wonder if I asked the question out loud, even. Maybe I asked it in my head. Which is definitely where it should stay.

I've heard of runners hallucinating when they run really long distances. I didn't run all that long or far, but maybe it happens sooner for thirteen-year-olds.

I can't blame it on food this time. Chrissy brought me some leftover soft tacos with chicken and guacamole. And I ate every crumb, since all of it was good for my body.

But then, finally, Pop lets out this long, tired breath and says, "I don't know, Leta. I don't think he's sent your mom money for a long time." I don't exactly know what he means until he says, almost to himself, "Never wanted her to work, but he wouldn't send her a penny."

I think he's saying that all these years Dad's worked out of state, Mom's never gotten any of the money. How did she take care of me and Amelia?

I'm surprised by the wild, wicked flash of my anger. I swallow the lightning, though, because I don't want to say anything else.

Pop turns onto the last road home and says, "If you and Amelia were my daughters, I'd make sure you had everything you needed and wanted. Some dads just don't know what they have, I guess."

I watch the cornfields until we're home.

Mom knocks on my bedroom door. It's not closed, but I guess Mom understands rooms are private things.

I close my book. Mom smiles at me. "What are you reading?"

I hold it up. *Summer Sisters.* I have a thing for Judy Blume, even if her books were written way before I was born.

Mom smiles but doesn't say anything about the book. Instead she says, "How's your foot?"

It's actually feeling a lot better. I can almost walk without a limp.

To Mom, I just say, "It feels great."

Maybe Mom sees something different on my face, because she says, "I don't want you to run if it's still hurting, Leta."

Did Pop tell her something? He promised not to. Does she know I might have a stress fracture?

Pop wouldn't betray me like that, would he?

I swallow hard and say, "It's fine. Really. It was just a little sore."

"Pop said you're still pool running."

"Yeah. It saves my joints for the big race. Especially the ones in my foot." When did it become so easy to lie?

Mom nods. "I'm sure you'll be a star."

She looks like she means it.

I will myself to believe her.

"Do you have a minute?" Mom asks, still hanging around in my doorway.

"Sure," I say. My stomach clenches like it knows more than I do.

Mom gestures toward the kitchen with her head. "I wanted to talk to you and Amelia about something."

My mouth goes dry. I know what it is before she says a word. But still I follow her to the kitchen. Still I sit in my seat across from Amelia.

Still I try to process the words "Your dad and I are getting a divorce."

Everything goes a little hazy after that.

I'm pretty sure Mom says something like "I didn't want to tell you right before your big meet," even though she *has* told me right before my big meet. I'm pretty sure she says something about Dad's other life and another woman. I'm pretty sure Mom adds, "I just didn't want to keep it from you."

I feel sick to my stomach. I wish she'd kept it from us. I wish she'd let me live in my fantasy world where I could fix everything by winning the district title for the four-hundred-meter dash. Hope needs a little help sometimes, you know? And what does it have now?

I feel Amelia's eyes on me. I blink hard. She's not crying; why should I?

"I'm sorry," Mom says, eyes glassy, shoulders slumped forward like she's trying to protect her heart.

I want to tell her it's not her fault. I want to say I understand. I want to let her know I know she did everything she could. But all those words get stuck in my throat.

What comes out instead is "What about Amelia's daddy-daughter dance?"

Mom looks at me strangely. "What do you mean, what about—"

"Who's gonna take Amelia to the daddy-daughter dance?"

Silence hangs around us until Mom says, "Pop will take her. Just like last year."

But I don't want Pop to take her. I want Dad to take her. I want Amelia to know she matters to Dad, she's important, she deserves every good thing in life.

Amelia starts talking about the dance then—the dress she'll wear, how she wants her hair (will I braid it for her?), whether Pop will take her out to eat at McDonald's first. Why does it matter so much to me when it doesn't seem to matter anymore to Amelia?

Maybe because I never got a daddy-daughter dance either. And maybe I needed to know I mattered to Dad, that I was important, that I deserved and still deserve every good thing in life.

I slip away from the table and close myself in the bathroom and stare at myself and wonder, *Mom did enough, but did I?*

And just like it knows the answer to my question, my foot starts throbbing again.

Thirty-five

THURSDAY

I don't say anything to Chrissy and Raina at school, and they don't ask why I'm being so quiet.

Sabrina's the first one I would usually talk to about things like this, but she's not interested in being a friend anymore. I watch her from across the field. She sits in the sun with Briana and Brooke. It must be uncomfortable without shade, but she doesn't seem to care.

My eyes snag on Natalie, sitting alone in the same place she always sits. There's a spot at our picnic table. Why haven't we invited her to sit with us?

Have we been saving a place for Sabrina, who will probably never come back?

I make a split-second decision and shove away from the

picnic table, walk to Natalie, and invite her to sit with us.

She looks at the table and back at me. She doesn't say anything, just picks up her lunch and follows me to Chrissy and Raina.

I try not to notice their wide-open mouths.

"No one likes to eat alone," I say. "And we have an extra place at the table."

I introduce her to Chrissy and Raina, like we don't all already know each other.

"Hi, Natalie," Chrissy says.

"Hi, Natalie," Raina echoes.

Natalie smiles at her sandwich and says hello back.

Across the field, I feel Sabrina's eyes burning my back.

I wonder what kind of list she'll volunteer me for this time.

The whole day, I carry my secret the way I carry my period supplies: close, hidden, and unwanted. (Displaying them today lasted a whole two hours. I heard some boys snickering and packed them up real fast.)

The whole day, I feel like bursting. I wobble. I lean. I limp. The whole day, I bite my tongue.

No one wants to know about how my world is falling apart.

Right before the last bell rings, dismissing us from Pre-Algebra, someone leans over and whispers, "Thank you for inviting me to sit with you at lunch."

I look right into Natalie's dark brown eyes. I shrug and repeat what I said at lunch. "No one likes eating alone."

Natalie nods. "I didn't ask to move here," she says. It's so soft I wonder if she's actually talking to herself. She clears her throat. "I guess that's just what happens when your parents get divorced." And, softer: "Everything changes."

Numbers swim in front of my eyes. The bell rings. I shove my book into my backpack and rush out of the room so fast I collide with Benny Dunlap.

"Sorry," I mumble.

He waves a hand. "No worries."

A friend of his, Colton Farris, elbows him. "Better go wash that stench off your shoulder, Benny," he says. "If that shirt's as old and smelly as her shoes, no one will want to run behind you."

My face ignites. When I look back at Natalie, her eyes laser into me, unpeeling layers, uncovering secrets, undoing the walls I've worked so, so hard to build.

I fly down the hall before I'm the one who breaks.

Thirty-six

THURSDAY

When Pop and I get to the pool this afternoon, it's locked. Pop bangs on it a couple of times, but it looks like no one's around. He pulls out his phone and punches in some numbers. When he's done talking to the person on the other end, he sighs and looks at me. "Pool's closed on Thursdays for cleaning," he says. "Don't know how I missed that."

I needed to run today, even if it was in the pool.

"Guess it won't hurt to sit out a day," Pop says.

"NO!" The word practically tears out of me. I feel my throat rip. My mouth might be bleeding. I press a hand to my lips.

Pop gapes at me. I've never talked to him like that before.

But if I sit out today, I won't win district. Don't ask me how I know that. I just do.

"Take me back to practice," I say.

Pop shakes his head. "You can't run on that foot, Leta."

I don't care. I need to run. So I say again, "Take me back to practice, Pop."

Pop stares at me for what feels like a very long time. Finally he says, "Okay," and heads toward his car.

I watch his back for a second before following him, trying my best not to limp.

I know I haven't won that easily. But Pop drives me back to practice and even walks me all the way to the track.

Turns out Pop wasn't walking me to the track just to be nice.

As soon as we reach Coach Mac, he says, "Tell her she can't run on that foot today."

Coach Mac looks surprised to see us. "What happened to the pool?"

"It was closed," Pop says. "For cleaning."

"Huh," Coach Mac says.

"And Leta still wants to run," Pop says.

"Well, she can't," Coach Mac says. She looks at me when she says, "She has to save her foot for the big race."

"But how am I supposed to win if I miss another day of practice?" My throat feels tight, and you can hear it in my words.

I don't even know if I can run a four hundred anymore. I know it's only been five days since I ran the last one, but five days is an eternity in running fitness.

"One day isn't gonna hurt you," Coach Mac says.

"That's what I told her," Pop says.

They don't understand. They don't know how important this is to me.

My stomach rolls. I'm going to throw up, and my throat's too tight and fiery to say anything.

And then I hear someone say, "I have a pool you can use."

Natalie. She looks right at Coach Mac. "At my house. We have a pool. It's deep."

Coach Mac looks from one of us to the other. Her eyes settle on me. She sighs. "Fine," she says. Her eyes move to Natalie. "But only if your parents say it's okay."

"It's just my mom," Natalie says. "I'm sure it will be fine."

Coach Mac waves a hand. "All right." She points at me. "You only run in water. Not on land. Not until Saturday."

I swallow hard and nod.

Natalie says, "I'll go with them. Show them where I live." She points. "It's not very far."

Coach Mac sighs again. "I could get in trouble for this," she says to no one. Then she turns her back like she doesn't want to see us walk away, get in Pop's car, and drive off.

Natalie's pool is nice. Concrete bottom, rocky surface, and even a waterfall on one side of it.

Her house looks like a tiny log cabin, with dark green shutters and a front door to match. It has the kind of wraparound porch Mom would love, with two rocking chairs on one side of the door and a polished wooden swing on the other.

I think about what it would be like, living in a house like this. Natalie probably never has to worry about whether she'll have enough food to eat. And she gets a pool right outside her door. She probably has her own room.

But I bet she'd give it all up to have her dad back.

Same as me.

No one talked about how Natalie would get back to practice. So when Pop says, "Natalie? You want to train in the pool? This is your race, too," Natalie looks at me.

She's not asking permission. She's just trying to read my reaction. And even though I feel a little like Pop has betrayed me, offering training secrets to the competition, I try to smooth out any frown wrinkles on my face.

I don't care is what I hope she sees.

We're a sisterhood, I remind myself. *We can compete against each other, but that doesn't mean we don't also lift each other up. Help each other out. Defend each other.*

I've been thinking a lot about this, and I think I'm starting to understand. One wins, we all win. It's hard to remember, when you're in the middle of a race, but I'm trying. And I think that's what counts.

After a second Natalie says, "Okay. Sure."

Pop tells her she needs a belt like mine, or some kind of flotation device, and she disappears into the house. She comes back out with what looks like foam weights.

"My mom does water aerobics," she says.

"Perfect," Pop says.

And then, for an hour and a half, he makes us run water intervals, yelling out, "Curve, straight, curve, home stretch!"

We run thirty-two, side by side, legs scissoring the water, barely making a ripple. Pop's fast running music blares from the Bluetooth speaker.

By the time we're done, the sun's starting to sink, and Natalie's two sisters—one older, one younger—stand on the stone edge, watching us, cheering us home.

It almost feels like a meet. Except there are no winners and losers, just two runners pretend-running because they love it and they're a team.

Before I leave I make sure to tell Natalie thank you.

She dips her head. "It was fun. Your grandpa is something else."

"You should see him when he runs."

Natalie nods and smiles so big I can see practically every single square of her braces. "I think I've heard stories." Which doesn't make me feel embarrassed at all. It makes me smile instead.

I start to turn away, but Natalie says, "Maybe we can do this again sometime. It's a nice change from running round and round a track."

"Going nowhere in a pool?" I say.

Natalie laughs. "They say gravity's an enemy."

Pop and Natalie's mom join us. Pop laughs too. "You're not wrong about that."

"How are you still running?" Natalie's mom says to Pop. "At your age? I can hardly jog a mile."

Pop's laugh only gets louder. "I guess when you run

because you love it, your bones and joints don't get so whiny. You can run forever."

He'll be running forever. I hope I will too.

Natalie's mom puts her arm around Natalie. "That's what Natalie wants to do," she says. "Run forever."

Natalie's eyes shine, and she drops them to the ground, blinking hard.

Does she want to run forever, or does she want to run away forever? And if she wants to run away, what is she running away from?

I don't have time to figure it out. Pop says, "Well, I better get Leta home. Her mother's a little particular about sleep."

Natalie's mom says, "Wait just a minute," and disappears inside the house. She comes out with a plastic bag full of chocolate chip cookies. "I hear pool running makes you hungry," she says with a grin.

I eat three of them before we even back out of the driveway. (It's a long driveway.)

I hate to say it, but they're way better than Mom's.

Once Mom forgot how much sugar she put in her cookie dough. And once she thought she'd mixed in baking soda, but the cookies came out looking like flat pancakes. Another time she meant to double a recipe and accidentally only doubled the butter and sugar. They were the greasiest, butteriest cookies the world has ever seen before.

I'm not saying I didn't still eat them. A cookie's a cookie.

But Mom should take a few lessons from Natalie's mom.

Thirty-seven

THURSDAY

Pop pulls into my driveway, but he doesn't unlock the doors. I'm about to do it myself when he says, "Hang on, Leta."

"Aren't you coming inside?" Pop usually eats with us on Thursday nights.

He shakes his head. "I told your mother I had a date."

The way he says it makes me wonder if he does have a date or if he just told Mom that to get out of dinner with us. I don't ask. Maybe it's not my business. And maybe I don't want to know, really.

"I have something for you." He twists toward the back seat and hands me a package before glancing at the front door.

"What's this?"

"Just open it." Pop flutters his hands. "And don't tell your mother."

I tear off the wrapping and pull out a shoebox. My breath catches in my throat, and when I lift the lid, I almost screech.

I've never, ever, ever had brand-new track shoes.

"I thought you could use shoes that don't flap at you while you're running." Pop tries to smile, but it looks sad. "Track spikes can only help so much."

He can't afford these any more than Mom can. How in the world did he get them?

I wonder if I should tell him I can't take them. But he's looking at me with such hope and sadness, I can't quite do it.

Instead, I breathe, "Thank you."

"You win in those old, ratty things," Pop says. "Just think what you can do in these."

Just think.

I hug him so tight I have to remind myself not to break him.

I stuff the shoes in my backpack, head straight to my room, and slide them under some blankets in my closet. Mom will see them at the meet, but by then it will be too late to make me give them back. You can't give back shoes you've already run in. All that sweat and...

Ew. I don't want to think about another person's sweat inside my old shoes.

You're not supposed to wear new shoes in an important race, but in my case it's okay. After all, who knows when those old, smelly things would fall apart for good? These new shoes will protect my feet. They have more spring and cushion. It's only a lap around the track.

And with a still-aching foot, I need all the help I can get.

I uncover the box and look at the shoes again one more time. They're gray and white, with fluorescent pink and yellow markings and white laces. They're the best shoes I've ever had. And they don't smell. I get to make them smell, not someone else.

I shove my old shoes past some pairs I don't wear anymore because they're too tight. I re-hide the new box just in time.

Mom taps on the door. I bolt out of the closet. "I was just... picking out what I'm wearing tomorrow," I say.

Mom raises an eyebrow at me. It was weird, I know. I don't usually pick out what I'm wearing for school the next day. I don't have enough clothes to pick anything out. I wear what's clean.

"You haven't had supper, have you?" Mom says.

"No." But I ate six cookies. Maybe more.

"Oh," Mom says. She looks surprised. Was she expecting me to eat with Pop? Did they make that arrangement and he forgot? But he usually eats with *us* on Thursday nights. Confusion whispers all kinds of things, but the loudest of them is *There's not enough food. She's worried because there's not enough food.*

Maybe Mom sees the worry on my face, because she says, "Usually you come home starving." She smiles before turning. "Your plate's waiting in the microwave."

I guess there is enough food. My breath heaves out in a loud gust.

It's only when Mom turns and walks off that I realize how close I came to giving away the secret of my new shoes. Heat spreads over me, followed by an icy cold.

I don't like secrets. But sometimes they're necessary.

I follow Mom out and eat two plates of Hamburger Helper, for good measure.

Runners need their fuel.

The truth is, I don't really understand why Pop and I have to keep those new shoes a secret. Pop paid for them; he didn't steal them. Maybe it has something to do with Mom needing to raise two daughters on her own. Maybe she needs to prove something to herself and the world.

And I guess I can understand that a little bit. So the shoes stay a secret.

I don't take them out again that night, especially since Amelia's always around and watching, and she has a loud mouth and can't keep secrets.

I dream about them instead, along with the list I'll make now.

Girls with the Coolest Shoes.

Thirty-eight

FRIDAY

Natalie sits with us at lunch the next day. Chrissy and Raina chatter about the meet, but Natalie's as quiet as I am.

After a while, Natalie says, "How's your foot, Leta?"

For a second I wonder why she's asking. Does she want to know so she can feel more confident about beating me tomorrow? Does she want to know so she can plan how hard she'll run to steal my district champion title?

My stomach knots up tight. My voice sounds high and strangled when I say, "It's fine. Healed, I think."

She looks at me like she doesn't quite believe me, but Raina and Chrissy say, "That's great!" and "You'll be able to run in the relay!"

They're all so focused on me, no one notices Sabrina, Briana, and Brooke walk by, stop, and turn back.

"Hanging out with your competition, Leta?" Brooke says. She looks innocent, like she's just asked a non-loaded question. But Brooke has all kinds of hidden depths. I mean, we all do. She's just a little better at spreading innocence over her shadowy places. Money does that, I guess.

I don't want to admit that she's gotten to me, but my throat goes completely dry and scratchy. I glance at Natalie. She stares at the table, tracing words someone carved in it a long time ago, probably. It takes me a while to say, "Not everything's a competition, you know." It sounds like I haven't used my voice in a thousand years.

Do I really mean it? I don't have time to figure that out before Brooke says, "That sounds like something losers say." She leans closer, like she's about to tell us a secret. "Everything's a competition." She gestures toward Sabrina. "See? I won your former best friend."

Sabrina stares at her shoes and doesn't say anything at all. My face burns so hot I'm surprised it doesn't disintegrate. That same hot feeling moves from my chest to my throat, and I can't stop the words from spilling right out. "She wasn't my best friend."

So much for a sisterhood.

Everybody has a match. We all have the ability to burn it

to the ground. We all have the capacity to destroy it.

Sabrina lifts her eyes now, meets mine for a second, and turns away. Brooke and Briana start to follow her, but she turns back to say, "Hope you don't end up on any more embarrassing lists." The way she says it makes it clear she hopes the exact opposite will happen.

And maybe she'll be the one to put me there. Again.

If a hole could open up right here in the field and swallow me, I would barely waste time welcoming it. I would just jump right in.

Raina and Chrissy stare at me, open-mouthed.

I don't want to do any more damage than I've already done, so I mumble something about needing to go to the library and head toward the school doors.

"Leta. Wait."

I stop, close my eyes, and take a deep breath. Why does she have to be everywhere?

"It's not right," Natalie says. "Those lists."

What does she know about it? I don't even turn around.

"You should tell someone," she says. "That's harassment."

Now I start walking. She obviously doesn't understand how it works in this school. The important people—boys or girls—never get in trouble. They can tear people to shreds and pretend like it's just a regular old day.

"Leta," Natalie says.

I keep on walking.

"Let someone else sort it out," I want to say. "I'm not the only one on those lists," I want to say. "It's not harassment; it's just the way the world works for people like me," I want to say.

But every step I take feels heavier and heavier, like my shoulders know the truth.

Coach Mac doesn't have us do anything in athletics except watch the Barbie movie. Which would have been nice earlier in the week, during my heaviest flow days. Day four of my period isn't so bad. Hardly a trickle. I won't even notice it tomorrow—which is a good thing.

We don't get to watch the whole thing, but the half of it we see is . . . eye-opening, I guess. The Barbies operate like a real sisterhood. They want what's best for everyone. They don't tear each other down or criticize or judge each other or make stupid lists like they're all in competition for some vague prize no one's ever seen. They're powerful because they stand with each other. Their voices are important and can be heard because they lift each other up. They are stronger together.

I glance at Sabrina and Brooke and Briana. I wonder if they see the same things or if a sisterhood is just too impossible to build in the real world.

Thirty-nine

FRIDAY

I maneuver the bus stairs carefully since I don't want to hurt my foot, and by the time I get down the three of them, Amelia's already halfway down the driveway, headed toward her friends' house.

"Amelia!"

Mom told me Amelia needed to come home with me today. She told me I needed to "make sure" Amelia came home with me today. I know she told Amelia the same thing this morning. I remember Amelia arguing with her.

At first I think Amelia's not going to stop and I'll have to walk all the way to her friends' house, knock on the door, and drag her back home. But then she stops, turns around, and glares at me.

"What?"

Attitude! What's gotten into Amelia? Where did my sweet (if a little wild) sister go?

I just say, "Mom said you're supposed to come straight home today."

"Well, Mom's not here." Amelia folds her arms across her chest and juts out a hip. We've been here before. I feel like I have déjà vu.

"So? I am."

Amelia narrows her eyes at me. "So?"

"So? Mom told me to make sure you come home."

"I want to go to my friends' house." Amelia switches to her other hip.

"You can't."

"Yes, I can."

"No. You can't." Now I'm starting to get mad.

Amelia stares at me, and I stare back at her. We're having a staring contest. Who will blink first? Amelia does. So I say, "What's so special about your friends' house, anyway?"

We keep staring at each other, me hoping Amelia won't take off running somewhere I can't follow, Amelia hoping . . . well, I don't know. I'm not sure I know my sister anymore. Too much is changing.

Why is everything changing?

After a minute, at least, of staring at each other, Amelia says, "Fine." Then: "I hate you, Leta."

I wonder if she knows how much those words hurt.

I heard the lock click before I could do anything about it.

She took the key, too.

So now I'm out on the porch, baking in the sun, with no way to call Mom while Amelia sits in the air-conditioned house reclining in the hallowed armchair. Last time I peeked in the window, she was stuffing her face with Spam and crackers.

Yes. More Spam. She must have a hidden stash of it.

She didn't even look my direction.

My stomach gives a mournful howl so loud Amelia can probably hear it inside. Sweat drips down my back. I can't even do my homework, since my arms have sweat glands, and I'd end up soaking the paper in minutes.

But if Amelia thinks the misery of being locked out will change my mind about letting her go back to her friends' when Mom already said it's not allowed, she's wrong.

So I sit out here, melting, while she sits comfortably inside, a queen in a comfy chair.

Like I said, sometimes it's hard to tell who the winner is.

Amelia unlocks the door half an hour before Mom's supposed to get home, probably because someone has to make supper and she's never bothered to learn how.

She doesn't want me to act like her mom, but what am I supposed to do when she acts helpless—falls asleep in the closet when the bus is already on its way? Does zero homework and prefers instead to watch cartoons on Netflix? Doesn't even cook herself supper? Doesn't she know Spam in a can isn't supper? It may keep her alive, barely, but it won't give her the nutrients she needs.

I slam cookie sheets around. Amelia doesn't move from her spot on the recliner. The anger wells up so hot in me that I finally say, "Don't you want to learn how to cook for yourself? So I don't have to act like your mom?"

Amelia narrows her eyes at me, then flicks them back to the screen. "Don't you want to learn how to be a sister? So I don't have to listen to another mom who's not really my mom?"

The words sting. I turn away.

"Fine," I say.

"Fine," she says.

Barbie didn't have a sister. I bet that's why she didn't have all this rage in her.

The silence hangs over us like an angry cloud. Even Mom feels it, I guess, because as soon as she walks in the door, she looks from one of us to another. "What happened?" she says. Her eyes look worried.

"Nothing," Amelia and I say at the same time. Which probably tells Mom all she needs to know.

Mom looks too tired to ask more. She hardly eats a thing. Sometimes I wonder why I do anything at all.

I try to go to bed early so I can get the sleep Pop always says runners need before a big, important race, but Amelia keeps her lamp on, pretending to read.

And I don't say anything, because maybe I'm still mad, and I don't want to give her the satisfaction of knowing she's bothering me.

I turn my face to the window and squeeze my eyes shut.

Finally, thirty minutes after getting into bed, I say, "Good night, Amelia."

She doesn't say anything.

"Love you."

No response.

"Sweet dreams."

Nothing.

"See you in the morning."

Complete silence.

She keeps her light blazing all night.

Nothing is turning out the way it's supposed to.

I hope that doesn't include tomorrow's track meet.

Forty

SATURDAY

Mom shakes me awake. I must have slept through my alarm, probably because of Amelia's blazing light, which I finally turned off sometime last night once she fell asleep.

"Leta," Mom whispers. "Pop will be here in half an hour."

I bolt straight up.

I already packed my bag last night, including the new track shoes Pop bought me and some period supplies for the last little trickles. Mom told me I could still wear a tampon, even if my flow was light. She even bought some special "light flow" tampons for me.

"It'll be better than running an important race in a pad," she said. And I'm sure she's right—especially with those hand-me-down uniforms that are tight in all the wrong places because they were made for boys.

Also, pads and sweat don't mix well. And you wouldn't believe how sweaty your underwear gets when you run on a regular April day. They should make special period supplies for athletes. Because what if we don't want to wear tampons?

I hustle through the house because I still need to shower and eat an orange or a banana or something. Nothing too heavy. But something to give me energy.

Mom's waiting at the front door when I get out of the bathroom, a banana and a brown sack in her hand.

"Pop's here," she says. "I packed you some breakfast and some snacks."

"Thanks, Mom."

She hugs me tight. "We'll be there before your race. Run fast. For yourself and no one else."

The words unbalance me. They sound like something Pop would say. Have they been talking about me?

But when I glance back at her, Mom's already moving away, toward her room. Probably to get a little more sleep before making the long drive to Beeville.

Before climbing into Pop's car, I peel the banana and stuff some in my mouth so my words stay put.

I don't even taste it.

Coach Mac has a small TV rigged up at the front of the bus.

"What's this?" Chrissy asks as we move up the steps.

"Figured I'd let you girls watch the rest of the Barbie movie on the way," Coach Mac says. She waves her phone. "I can stream it from here."

It's too early to watch a movie, but I have to admit, I'm interested in seeing the rest of it.

Raina and Chrissy drop into a seat. Raina claps her hands. "I can't believe she's letting us watch a movie." Coach Mac usually has us sit in mostly silence, thinking about our races.

But I guess this movie is important to her. Maybe it's all the sisterhood references.

"It's so good," Chrissy says. She sighs. "I loved Barbie."

I loved Barbie too. I still have some in a box in my closet. Pop used to buy me a new one every year at Christmas.

Someone giggles behind us. I glance over my shoulder. Brooke and Briana huddle together. Sabrina's not on the bus yet.

I ignore them. I'm still not sure what you're supposed to do with people like Brooke and Briana when you're trying to build a sisterhood, but maybe you learn along the way. I have Raina and Chrissy. And maybe even Natalie.

Natalie steps onto the bus. I wave at her and hope she takes it to mean *Sit with me*. She stares at me for a minute before heading our direction. I scoot toward the window, and she drops down beside me.

"Coach Mac says we're watching the Barbie movie on the way," I say.

"Yeah. That's what she told me when I got on the bus," Natalie says. "It's a great movie. My sisters and mom and I watched it in the theater when it came out."

I feel a twinge of jealousy. It's been a long, long time since Mom and Amelia and I watched anything in a theater. But I push the feeling away. It doesn't belong in a sisterhood.

I think about what Pop has always told me, "Every feeling is valid. Let yourself feel what you feel. But make sure you do the right thing with the feeling."

"That sounds really fun," I say to Natalie.

And I think that's the right thing to do with the feeling.

There's a quote in the Barbie movie that stayed with me. The woman who plays Ruth Handler, the creator of Barbie, says it. She says, "We mothers stand still so our daughters can look back and see how far they've come."

It makes me think of Mom and all she does for me and Amelia. And how she'll probably be the loser in her divorce.

How she already has been in the separation. It's not fair. But maybe it won't be like that forever.

Mom's life isn't exactly what she wanted or expected. But she stayed. And she's here. So Amelia and I can have the world.

I write her a great big *Thank you* on a sheet of notebook paper. It's nothing fancy, but it doesn't need to be.

I press it into the bottom of my bag, saved for later.

Forty-one

SATURDAY

I don't eat any of the snacks Mom packed me. My stomach is too queasy thinking about my race.

And finally, right before ten, they call the four hundred.

They split us into three heats since every school in the district is here. Most schools have only one runner, but a few, like ours, have two.

Natalie isn't in my heat. She's in the first one, I'm in the third one.

The top eight finishers, based on their times, will race in the final at one.

More waiting. But time to rest my legs.

Natalie crosses the finish line first in her heat. Two long-legged girls cross the finish line almost tied in the next one.

And then it's my turn.

My heart hammers my chest as I set up in the starting blocks. I'm in lane two, which isn't as good as lane one. My new shoes shine.

"On your mark!"

I glance up at the stands, where Mom and Pop and Amelia stare at the staggered starting line.

"Get set!"

Always looking for Dad.

The gun fires, and I take off.

I hardly notice the pain in my foot. I have two good races in me, don't I? Maybe three?

My chant matches my stride.

Please please please please please

I run just hard enough to stay ahead of the others. I need to save myself and my foot for the finals.

I round the first corner and find my stride.

It's not until I'm done with the straightaway that my lungs start burning, not until the last curve that my legs turn mushy, not until the final stretch into home that I hear the shouts.

"Faster!"

"Kick it in now!"

"Move those legs!"

I pretend they're all yelling at me. I speed up just a little—enough to cross the line a few seconds before the others.

Coach Mac holds up her stopwatch, squints at the number, and crosses the lanes to me.

"You'll have to do better than that time in the finals," she says, real low like she doesn't want anyone else to hear. That's how I know I made it to the finals.

I nod but don't tell her I was holding back on purpose, trying to protect my foot. She'd probably understand, but you never know.

I've worked too hard to sit out.

I need to run.

I need to win.

I head toward the bleachers, where Mom and Pop stand talking with a woman. I squint. It's Natalie's mom.

"Good race, Leta," someone calls from the grassy area inside the track. It's Natalie.

"Thanks," I say.

I wonder if I'll ever feel big enough to tell her the same.

Maybe I'm the one who poisons the sisterhood.

A list waits for me back at the tent. This one is titled *Girls with Boy Bodies*. Natalie, Chrissy, and I made the list.

I don't know who wrote it or who put it right next to my snacks, like they wanted me to see it.

"Hey, Leta. Good race." Benny stands outside the girls' tent, a Gatorade bottle in one hand. Green, the worst kind. I shove the list into my backpack so he doesn't see it.

My face burns just thinking he may have already seen it.

He ran his final earlier. He finished fourth, so I'm not sure what to say other than "Thanks, Benny." He can't be happy with fourth.

He stands there for a minute, like maybe he's waiting for something or he has something more to say. The silence makes my face burn even hotter. Finally he says, "Good luck in the finals."

He still has the eight-hundred-meter relay left, so I say, "Good luck in the relay."

He smiles. My heart does a little flip-flop.

I pretend to have something important to find in my backpack, and when I look up again, Benny has disappeared.

I show Chrissy the list. She tears it in half. Her eyes look fierce.

"If I had a boy body, this uniform wouldn't keep riding

up my butt," she says. She punctuates the words with a very theatrical wedgie-picking, which makes me and Raina burst out laughing.

"These lists are stupid," Raina says. "Boys trying to have power over girls." She sounds like her grandma. Her grandma's a lot like Mom. Which is awesome but also a little disheartening because they're a whole generation apart. I know progress is slow, but decades slow? Generations slow? How sad is that?

Raina's words make me think about Sabrina. "And girls trying to have power over girls," I say, and I almost immediately regret it.

Raina and Chrissy stare at me. I bet they're thinking about Sabrina too.

"Why?" I don't mean to ask the question. I don't think anyone here can answer it.

"My sisters have theories about that." Natalie sits on one of the mats, untying her shoes. She shakes one of them out, like maybe she picked up a pebble or something.

"We're listening," Chrissy says.

Natalie looks up at us. "They say that because there's only so much room for women at the top, we all have to compete against each other to get there." She shrugs. "So if we tear another girl down, we get a little closer to the top."

"That's not a sisterhood," I say. "That's a . . ."

I don't even know what to call it.

"Yeah," Natalie says. "I know."

I think about the way I've treated her. That's not a sisterhood either. I'd like to apologize, but the words feel sticky and impossible. We still have a race to run. Anything can happen.

There's only so much room at the top. And I'm not sure how to not care about that. Because the top is what brings your dad home.

Forty-two

SATURDAY

I don't eat any lunch. When Pop tries to convince me to, treating me to his lecture about how a runner needs fuel to run fast, I tell him I'd rather run on an empty stomach than one that's sloshing around with half-digested matter. Which is 100 percent true. I'm eating, just not right before the race. Blech.

I guess he can't think of an argument, because he only says, "Well, make sure you eat after the finals, then. You still have the relay."

Do I have another two four hundreds in me?

I guess we'll see.

Pop stands there a minute, looking just like Benny. He opens his mouth, closes it, opens it again. Finally, he manages to say, "Well, good luck in the finals. I know you can do it, Leta Lightning Laurel." And then he says something weird, under his breath but still loud enough for me to hear.

"Long as you keep your eyes on the track."

I chalk it up to Pop being Pop.

They call the final for the four hundred. I walk toward the starting line on unsteady legs. I hope they get steadier once the race starts, or I won't be able to manage three steps, let alone a whole lap.

My foot throbs, but I ignore it.

This time I'm in lane one, the best place because you can see all the runners and gain some speed around the curves. It's way better than starting in lane eight, where you bolt off feeling like you're ahead, only to have two curves prove you really aren't.

We kneel in the blocks.

"On your mark!"

I glance up at the stands, meet Pop's eyes. He jabs a finger toward the track. His finger says, *Eyes on the track.*

"Get set!"

My eyes peel away and search for Dad. A brown head bobs into view. My eyes snag.

The gun goes off before I'm ready, so I start a split second late.

A split second is everything in this race.

So is footing, and my second step sends a knife of pain up the center of my foot.

I run as hard as I can anyway.

Around one curve, gaining on the girl in lane six, another in lane five, the one in lane two. I pass them before the track evens out, but Natalie's in lane eight. She looks impossibly far ahead. I set my sights on her back and will my feet and legs to move faster.

Down the straightaway, pass the girl in lane three, foot screaming like I imagine Coach Mac will be when it's just me and Natalie racing for the title.

Around the last curve, pass the girls in lane seven and lane four. Home stretch. It's just Natalie and me.

My legs turn rubbery, but I pound them anyway, trying to ignore the slicing pain in my foot. I have a little bit left, so I put in a final kick. Natalie keeps pace with me. And then, just before we cross the finish line, she kicks in another gear.

She crosses the line first.

Coach Mac holds me up.

My foot hurts so bad I don't know if I'll ever walk again.

But what hurts worse is second place. Reporters don't take pictures or write articles about second-place winners. Moms don't send those articles and pictures to missing dads for second-place winners. Dads don't come home for second-place winners.

"Great race," Coach Mac says. I blink hard and try my best not to cry. "Now let's tape you up. You think you can run the relay?"

"I don't know."

I don't know if I ever want to run again.

Natalie watches me from the other side of Coach Mac, biting one thumbnail. I don't look at her because I'm not sure if I can.

When she says, "Good race, Leta," I shake my head and hope she'll get the message.

Go away.

Before she walks away, I hear her say, "I'm sorry."

And it's not fair that she had to say those words to me. I wouldn't want to say them to the runner I beat.

But I can't make myself say, "Don't be sorry about winning. You deserve it. You ran hard."

Because who wanted it—needed it—more?

Forty-three

SATURDAY

District's not the end.

We have two weeks before a special region invitational meet Coach Mac organized with her select running club. The top two runners in each race qualified for the special meet. Two runners from each district in the region will compete at the meet.

Which means Natalie and I will race again in the four hundred.

Coach Mac says it's an unusual opportunity and a huge honor and something that could be good for our running future.

But if I can't be the best at the four hundred, what's the point?

On the way home Pop says, "So? How's your foot?"

I stare out the window and blink hard. "Okay."

The truth is, it hurts more than it did before the meet. But if I can't win district, I have to win at the invitational. It's my last chance.

Our relay team won first, but I didn't smile when a reporter snapped a picture of me, Natalie, Chrissy, and Raina. Natalie had a better split than I did in the relay, and besides, what does Dad care about a team effort?

I needed to do this alone, and I didn't.

Pop's voice is quiet when he says, "Seems like you're limping more. So I don't know if I believe you, Leta."

I shrug. Pop sighs.

After a minute he says, "What happened out there?"

The question makes my throat hurt.

I failed. That's what happened.

I don't answer him.

Pop says, "Leta?"

I still don't answer.

We drive in that thick, heavy silence almost all the way home.

But I should have known Pop wouldn't give up so easily. Just before we hit Edna, he says, "I saw you start late because you were looking up in the stands. What were you trying to find?"

I swallow hard and close my eyes. "Nothing." It's impossible to explain how I'm always searching for Dad. How I still believe, after everything that's happened, that he'll come home. How there's this hole inside my heart that aches whenever I think about him out in the world, forgetting all about us.

Pop probably already knows all that anyway. But he doesn't say anything about it. He only says, "We'll train in the pool again. Your foot won't touch the ground until the region meet."

And maybe it's the way he says it—so confident that I'll run well at the invitational when I choked today. Or maybe I'm just tired of all the pressure, tired of thinking about Dad, tired of trying to solve the problem of Amelia's dance, one week away, tired of trying to change everything with a stupid race, a stupid medal that probably won't mean anything in a few years.

All my anger torches my words. "It didn't work! I lost! I wasn't fast enough! I failed!"

Something else slides out, as much as I try to swallow it.

"How will Dad remember us now?"

Only the hum of the road surrounds us then.

Pop stays quiet for what seems like a long time. And when he finally speaks, his voice has turned soft and gentle. "Since when is second place losing? Failing?"

Since your dad proved it's all you'll ever be. Second place.

He's moving on without us. He picked someone else.

I manage to swallow all those words.

"Not too long ago, I asked you why you run," Pop says. "And you couldn't answer the question." He glances at me from the corner of his eye. "Seems to me you need to figure that out."

I watch the blurred night outside my window.

We're almost home. I can't wait to get out of this car. But it's like Pop knows. He starts driving slower.

"You have to figure out if you run to win or if you run because it's in you, deep inside, and you have to." He pauses. "That's where winning comes from." Another pause. "And you don't even have to win to run. I'm still running because I love it. Because it's in me. Because without it, something in my life would be missing."

What does Pop know about things in your life being

missing? I have a Dad-shaped hole in me. That's a big missing.

We're home now. I grab my backpack from the back seat.

Pop puts a hand on my arm long enough to say, "You can't run for someone else, Leta. You have to run for yourself. Running doesn't change other people. It changes you."

I don't say a word as I climb out of the car and slam the door.

Forty-four

SUNDAY

When I wake up on Sunday, my foot looks a little swollen. And I wince just putting pressure on it.

I limp past the living room, where Amelia's already sitting in the recliner. She looks at me like she's challenging me to do something about that, but I ignore her and move out to the porch and toward the shed, where my bike has probably grown all sorts of spiderwebs and become a house for spiders. But even that doesn't keep me from wheeling it out and pedaling toward the street.

If I can't run, I'll bike.

I turn onto the canal road, where I do my longer runs, and head for the end of it, where a long line of water stretches all the way to the highway.

I stare at the water for hours, Pop's words from yesterday twirling in my head.

If I came here looking for answers, that muddy water doesn't have a single one for me.

Mom doesn't get home until five. It's the first time I've seen her since yesterday because Pop and I got home late and Amelia and Mom were already in bed. So of course the first thing she says is, "That was some race yesterday, Leta. I'm so proud of you."

"For second place?"

I don't know why my words are so slippery. *Stay put*, I tell them.

Mom's head tilts. She looks at me for a long second before she says, "Yes. For second place." I huff. Mom's eyes narrow. "You're not proud of yourself?"

I look at the floor and shrug. "I didn't win."

"You're going to regionals."

"Not because I was the best."

Mom lets out a frustrated groan. "You don't have to be the best at everything, Leta."

Maybe I do.

Amelia peeks out from the living room. If I was in a different mood, I might use the opportunity to steal the recliner from her. She's been hogging it all day, and I really need to put my foot up.

But I don't want to sit in Dad's old chair. It will only remind me I've failed.

Mom's voice tears into my thoughts. "My god, Leta. What are you trying to prove? That you can keep running on a possibly fractured foot? That you can power through pain without it knocking you off your feet for a while? That you're perfectly fine when you're not?"

Her words set my chest on fire. I glare at her. She has it so wrong.

Mom's not finished. Her voice is softer when she says, "Or maybe you're trying to prove you're good enough to be loved."

I keep glaring, my throat tightening.

She doesn't know anything.

"But, Leta, the people who matter love you whether you're first place or second place or last place. We're proud of you just because."

Mom takes a step closer. "I'm sorry your dad left. I'm sorry he doesn't call or visit. I'm sorry he's moved on without us. I'm sorry—"

"Stop!" The word erupts out of me. "Stop!"

Mom doesn't stop. "I'm sorry he doesn't come watch you run, because it really is a glorious thing to see you work so hard at something that's so important to you. And watch you fly and look so free—"

"Stop!" My voice sounds shaky now. The world blurs.

"It's not your fault, Leta." Mom's arms reach out for me and pull me close. She smells like mango. "What a shame." She kisses the top of my head. "What a shame that he doesn't get to see what a magnificent daughter he has."

Mom's shoulder is soggy by the time she lets me go.

Forty-five

SUNDAY

Mom and Pop sit at the kitchen table. I can hear them from my room.

"It's not failing, you know," Pop says. "Everybody needs help sometimes."

Mom's voice sounds shaky when she says, "I wanted to do this on my own."

"You're not supposed to be doing it on your own," Pop says. "He's supposed to be helping you. And he's not. That's not your failure; it's his."

"But I'm the one who has to ask the government for help," Mom says.

"So what?" Pop says. "You're doing the best you can, and no one can argue any different."

"I don't want the girls to go hungry," Mom says. Her voice sounds like it's about to break.

"Well, they'd never go completely hungry," Pop says. "Between you and me, we'd never let them. But the government can help. It's not a failure. It doesn't have to be forever."

They're quiet for a while until I hear Pop say, "I'm proud of you, you know. For whatever that's worth. You've raised some pretty outstanding daughters all by yourself. Who can do that and still be such an outstanding person herself?"

Someone sniffs. I'm pretty sure it's Mom.

She really is outstanding. Amelia and I hit the jackpot when it comes to moms. And maybe it's time to tell her. And Pop, too.

I take out my letter project and start to write.

I sit in my closet, staring at my old track shoes.

I put them on and lace them up. My big toe pokes through a hole in the left one.

I take them off and set them beside the new ones Pop gave me. Mom never mentioned them. I guess she and Pop talked about it and worked out whatever feelings she had about them. The new ones already have scuffs on the toes. I trace the marks.

Maybe I should accept that my season's over. My foot

hurts bad enough to give up now. And what's the point?

"What are you trying to prove?" Mom asked.

That I'm unforgettable. That I'm exceptional. That I deserve a dad who loves me and remembers who I am and that I need him.

Mom and Pop are telling me I do deserve that love. And that I already am exceptional and unforgettable.

But how do you make yourself believe something that doesn't feel true?

"What are you doing?"

Amelia's voice makes me jump.

"Nothing." I shove the old track shoes back where they were and scoot around to face her.

She wrinkles her nose. "What's that smell?"

I glare at her. She can't smell the shoes all the way out there.

Amelia sits down beside me, half in the closet, half out. "Did your foot hurt when you ran yesterday?"

I tug on a piece of brown carpet. "Yeah. A little."

"Why'd you run, then?"

I sigh. "Because I wanted to win district."

"Why?"

Amelia's not usually interested in my reasons for doing

anything. But maybe she knows, somewhere deep down, that I did it not just for me but for her, too.

So I say, "I thought maybe I could bring Dad home for your daddy-daughter dance." Softer: "It was stupid."

"I already have a date," Amelia says. "Pop."

"But you said you wished Dad would come home in time for the dance," I remind her.

"I did?" Amelia shakes her head. "I don't remember saying that."

She did. But it's not important enough to argue about.

"Pop's a really good dancer," Amelia says.

"But he's not Dad," I say.

Amelia cocks her head. "I don't even know Dad."

And she's right. Dad was never around for her. I guess I forgot that.

Going to a daddy-daughter dance with Pop is way better than going with a stranger.

"Want to watch some *Pokémon*?" Amelia says.

I really hate that show. But I say, "You bet" anyway.

"I'll let you have the chair," Amelia says on our way out of our room. "You need some help getting there, Limpy Leta?"

I shove her out of the way and speed-walk—speed-limp—to the recliner. I've already pulled up the footrest by the time she races into the room.

But only because she let me win big.

Forty-six

MONDAY

It's only me, Natalie, Chrissy, Raina, and Sabrina at track practice now.

I haven't talked to Natalie since district, but we're still stretching partners. She hasn't tried to talk to me, either. Maybe she's waiting for me to forgive her for winning. I want to tell her it's not necessary to forgive her for winning. But for some reason the words still feel stuck.

Sabrina's the alternate for the relay team, but she also qualified for the invitational in the two-hundred-meter dash.

Without Briana and Brooke, she looks lonely. So I say, "Hey, Sabrina, want to stretch with me and Natalie?"

It'll take longer to get through all the stretches with

three of us doing them, but that's better than stretching with a boy.

Benny and his eight-hundred-meter-relay team made the invitational too. All five of them are here.

Every now and then I feel Benny's eyes on me. I try not to look at him. He's not the one who made those lists, but his friends are. And he didn't say anything to make them stop.

Sabrina joins Natalie and me, but she doesn't look at us. She mostly stares at the ground.

None of us talk.

My foot throbs, like it's trying to talk for us.

But my chest throbs more. And I don't think any amount of rest or pool running or elevating the injured limb will make it feel any better.

Pop shows up late. I've been waiting for him, since I still can't run on the track. Coach Mac doesn't want me to let my foot feel even a hint of gravity for at least the next ten days, she said.

That will give me one day of running on the track before the invitational meet—if my foot feels good enough to run.

Sabrina will practice with the relay team, in my position, until the last day. And then, if I can't run, they'll have to switch it up.

Pop puts his arm around me. "I'll bring her back in time for the cooldown stretches," he tells Coach Mac. We walk toward the parking lot. Before I get in the car, I stop, stare at the track, and watch Natalie hand off to Chrissy, Chrissy to Raina, Raina to Sabrina. They'll practice handoffs for the first half hour, then move to the actual running workouts.

"Leta? You okay?" Pop says.

No. I'm not. But instead of saying that, I say, "I have something I need to do."

I head back toward Coach Mac.

"Hey, Coach."

Coach Mac is surprised to see me. "Leta?"

Before she can say anything else, I say, "You know what, Coach? I think I'm gonna sit this one out."

Coach Mac folds her arms across her chest. "I know. You're pool running. Coach's orders."

"No. I mean . . ." I let the words trail off.

"You mean you want to watch practice instead of pool running? I know pool running can be really boring—"

"I mean sit the meet out."

Coach Mac opens her mouth, but nothing comes out. I try to think of something else to say, some reason I can give her. But all the words get tangled in my throat.

Finally Coach Mac says, "But you've worked so hard, Leta."

I have. But not for the right reasons. Not because I wanted to win for *me*. Because I wanted to win for *him*. There's a big difference.

Pop's words come back to me. *If you aren't enough without winning, you'll never be enough.*

I glance toward Raina and Natalie and Chrissy and Sabrina. "There's no guarantee my foot will be healed anyway," I say. "Maybe it's best to give someone else a chance."

"We'll assess that when we get to that crossroad," Coach Mac says.

"I don't want to bring them down." It's halfway the truth.

"You don't," Coach Mac says. "You never have. Leta, you're the best person this team has. And I don't mean just as a runner. I mean all-around person."

She's not making this any easier, and besides, she doesn't know the things I've thought about Natalie and done and said to her these last few weeks. So I finally say, "I guess I just feel like I need to sit this one out."

"Because of your foot?"

I shrug. Let her think what she needs to think.

"Tell you what," Coach Mac says. "Why don't you take a couple of days off to think about it? I'm not trying to push you. But this could be good for your high school running career."

After another minute I say, "Okay." But I've already thought about it. I'll still have a high school running career. Because I'll still work as hard as I possibly can. One meet isn't gonna change that.

Pop puts his arm around me on the way back to his car. When I look over my shoulder, Coach Mac watches us, worry flipping all the way across her face.

But I feel almost free.

It takes Pop only a few minutes of silence in the car to say, "I'm proud of you, Leta. That took some guts, quitting before the biggest race of the year."

My chest burns. "It's not the biggest race of the year," I say. My voice sounds like the pointy track spikes on the bottom of my new shoes. "And I didn't quit. I'm just taking some time off. For me."

Pop nods like he agrees. But after another minute he says, "It's easier to quit than try and fail."

What is he talking about?! *He's* the one who told me I should reevaluate why I'm running. So more words spill out of me. Angry and harsh. "I'm running to win, and I don't want to run to win anymore."

"There's nothing wrong with running to win," Pop says, eyes fixed on the road. He's afraid to look at me. He's afraid my eyes will shoot daggers into his and blind him.

Because WHAT?! Didn't he tell me there *was* something wrong with running to win a week ago? He can't make up his mind! Or maybe he doesn't even remember what he told me.

"Not if you're running to win for yourself and no one else," Pop says.

I stare out the window so I don't have to look at him now.

He isn't finished. "Seems to me you have a good chance of winning that invitational and catching the eye of high school and maybe even college coaches. Even with an injury. And that would be for *your* future, no one else's." He lets the words hang between us.

I blink hard, my throat thickening with something I can't name. Or maybe I don't want to name it. It's a collection of all kinds of things. Words like *He's probably right* and *Why is everything so confusing all the time?* and heavy things like fear and anger and sadness. And it also includes a lot of words I need to say but can't.

I'm afraid of this life without a dad.

I'm tired of trying to be Amelia's second mom.

I'm angry that I had to grow up so fast, that I can't just be a kid.

I swallow all of it down and hope it never comes back up.

Forty-seven

TUESDAY

"Seems to me you have some thinking to do," Pop said before I got out of the car.

I guess I did. I've thought all day, and tonight I think more.

I don't know how long I sit in my closet, staring at those track shoes—one pair fresh and bright and new; the other dirty, smelly, and falling apart.

I don't know how long I turn the questions over in my mind.

What if I ran because I love it?

What if I ran to discover my real self, the one that always seems to hide behind expectations and hopes and plans that don't always turn out like I want them to?

What if I ran for me?

I don't know what time it is when Mom knocks on my door to tell Amelia and me she has a headache and is going to bed early.

But I know I've *really* made my decision this time.

Forty-eight

WEDNESDAY

On Wednesday Amelia beats me out to the bus stop in the morning, like she finally decided today was the day she'd stop falling asleep in our closet. She hasn't done it all week, but it's probably too soon to tell if it will last or not.

I get a few extra minutes to myself in the house, and I stand there looking around the tiny kitchen at the table with its empty chairs, the dresser Mom calls a buffet shoved against the wall, with her calendar turned to April, her note about the district meet and the star that says, *Leta won the silver medal in the 400!*

It makes me smile.

When I get out to the bus stop, Amelia says, "It's about time. What took you so long?"

"Maybe I fell asleep in the closet."

Amelia rolls her eyes. "Please. I haven't done that in ages."

I don't mention I found her curled up in the closet last week.

"Did you bring your track shoes?" Amelia says.

The question makes me raise both my eyebrows. "I don't need my track shoes." I can hear the bus now, motor disrupting the quiet around us.

"Did you quit running?"

I take a deep breath. "No," I say. "I've decided—"

"Good," Amelia interrupts. The bus squeals to a stop in front of us. Amelia heads toward the steps but throws a glance and words behind her. "I like you better when you're running."

I stare at the back of Amelia's head, so lost in my thoughts I don't notice Benny slide into the seat across from me until he says, "Hey, Leta."

I tell my face to cool it, but it burns hot anyway. "Hey." I stare at my hands so I don't have to look at him.

He clears his throat, clasps and unclasps his hands. "Listen, I just wanted to say I'm sorry about those stupid lists."

Well, this is completely unexpected.

I shrug, like the lists are no big deal. Like I have a sense of humor. Why do I do that? The lists *are* a big deal. And I do have a sense of humor, but not about boys humiliating girls and other girls joining in.

But Benny's not completely responsible for the lists. So I say, "You didn't make them."

"But I didn't stop them either." Benny's hands grip each other tight. His knuckles are white. "At least, not at first."

I don't say anything.

"My dad always says you don't have to be the person responsible for a crime to be guilty of it," Benny says. "You just have to go along. Not stand up for what's right. Ignore the wrong."

Benny's dad is a veterinarian in town. He set up the county's first animal shelter two years ago. He tries to save all the dogs that are dumped out on the county roads and left on their own.

I swallow whatever's caught in my throat.

"Anyway." Benny rubs his hands on his legs now. I still don't look at him, since my face still has flames eating away at it. "I'm sorry." He stands but doesn't move back to his place. Any second now, Mrs. Malcolm will yell at him to sit down, since the bus is barreling down the highway. But he just stands there.

Finally I look up, confused about why he hasn't gone back to his seat. His eyes meet mine. "I turned in those lists. To Miss Rawley."

Miss Rawley is the junior high counselor.

I nod and manage a quiet "Thank you" before Benny heads back to his seat.

"Sit down, Mr. Dunlap!" Mrs. Malcolm yells. The predictability of it almost makes me laugh.

Nothing will probably happen to those boys who made the lists and the girls who helped them. But maybe, at the very least, they'll stop making them.

I think about how Coach Mac said boys can be part of the sisterhood too. I'm starting to think Benny Dunlap might have the same kind of bonobo attitude that's needed. No one harms your sister, and everyone is your sister.

Isn't that the same thing as standing up for what's right?

I'm wrong about nothing happening to those boys. Quentin Pierce, Ryan Hensley, and Weston Garner are all written up and have their parents called and told they'll have five days of detention for inappropriate bullying behavior. Even

Briana and Brooke and Sabrina get two days of detention for their part in it all.

No one but me knows who told.

At lunch, Benny sits at a different table with some cross-country runners and a boy who can program anything and another boy who runs a book club at school.

I hope turning in his friends didn't cause too much trouble for him. But I'm glad he did what he did. And I think he is too. He laughs and jokes with the kids at his table, and he looks more like himself than he has in a while.

Raina, Chrissy, and I don't mention the lists at lunch. But you can tell we all feel a little freer, knowing we won't make the next terrible list—because there won't be one.

Natalie's not here. She said she had something to do in the library, but I'm not sure if she really did or if she's just avoiding me. We still haven't cleared the air. I still haven't said what I need to say.

I'm trying.

Halfway through lunch Raina bursts out singing. It's terrible singing. Chrissy spontaneously dances. It's terrible dancing. And I sit with my legs stretched out for all to see, even though I haven't shaved in almost a week.

Forty-nine

WEDNESDAY

Pop's waiting with Coach Mac when I get to practice. He grins at me like he already knows the answer to Coach's question, which she asked as soon as I was close enough to hear her.

"What'd you decide?"

"I guess it's more pool running today," I say.

Coach Mac's face breaks into a smile. She pumps a fist in the air. "I knew you wanted that win."

She's almost right. I don't necessarily want the win. I mean, yeah, maybe I do. But I don't *need* it. And I think that's the difference.

I just want to run.

I follow Pop toward his car. Someone calls my name, and when I turn around, Sabrina stands there, shifting from foot to foot.

"Hey," she says.

"Hey, Sabrina," I say. I glance at Pop.

"I'll be in the car," he says. I nod to let him know I heard him.

I turn back to Sabrina, my stomach clenching and unclenching. We haven't talked since she laughed at those lists and added my name to one or several. Since she started hanging around Brooke and Briana. There's no telling what she'll say after all this time.

She kicks at something on the ground. "I'm sorry about those lists," she says.

It seems like she means it, but I don't tell her it's okay. I don't even tell her what I told Benny this morning, because Sabrina *did* make a list, technically. Or at least she helped make one.

Instead I say, "They made me feel terrible, you know."

She winces and shakes her head. "I don't know . . ." She pauses, looks up at the sky, and blinks hard. "I don't know what happened," she tells a puffy white cloud. "I just . . . cracked, I guess."

I'm not exactly sure what she's saying, so I don't say anything.

"My mom and dad got a divorce, and I guess . . ." Another pause, another look at the sky, like maybe it'll have some answers for her if she squints hard enough. "I guess I just wanted someone to hurt as much as I was hurting."

"So you picked me." Didn't she know I was hurting, too? I guess I didn't really talk about it, so how could she? My friends have no idea where things have gone since the last time Dad was home because I haven't said a word about it.

She didn't tell me about her parents either. I wonder why.

Maybe sometimes you grow apart without really knowing the reason.

Now Sabrina stares at the ground. There's not much to see, just asphalt and loose pebbles. "Yeah. I guess," she says.

"Well, it worked," I say. "It hurt." I'm not letting her off easily. She needs to know what it all did to me. She needs to know that's not how things work in a sisterhood.

"I'm sorry," Sabrina says. This time she looks at me when she says it.

"Okay," I say. I'm glad she's sorry, but that doesn't mean we're going to be friends again. "I'm glad you told me." I start to turn away but think of something else. I face Sabrina again. "You know, if we're a sisterhood, we can't do things like that to each other. Laugh about lists. Add girls' names to them. Spread rumors and tear each other down." There are a hundred other things girls do to each other in junior high. I don't have time to stand here and list them all.

Sabrina nods and looks at the ground again. "I know."

And I guess that's all that needs saying. I head back toward Pop, waiting in the car. I feel her eyes on me the whole way. And before I open my door, Sabrina says, "Hey, Leta?"

"Yeah?"

"Running doesn't bring dads home. But it helps you find a home."

Her words feel true. I swallow hard and nod. "Thanks, Sabrina."

She watches us drive away.

"What was that about?" Pop says.

"Just Sabrina apologizing for something." Pop doesn't want to know all the details of what happened with her, and I don't want to dwell on them.

The past isn't nearly as bright as the future.

"How many four hundreds today?" I say.

"Forty," Pop says. "The magic number." He cuts his eyes at me. "Think you can handle it?"

"I can handle anything."

Pop pumps his fist in the air and turns into the lot.

Fifty

WEDNESDAY

Mom's not late picking me up for maybe the first time ever. She smiles at me when I get in the car. I smile back. "This the Leta I get when I'm on time?" she says.

"What do you mean?" I say. I glance at Amelia in the back seat. She's staring out the window like I'm not here. I don't know if she's actually ignoring us or if she's listening in and working really hard to pretend like she's not. Sisters are hard to read sometimes.

"You're usually not very happy with me."

"I worry when you're late."

"I know. I'm sorry." Mom smooths the hair on the back of my head but almost immediately pulls her hand away. "Ew. I forgot how sweaty you get, even in the pool."

My hair's very wet. And not from pool water. "You'd think the water would help, but it really doesn't," I say.

Mom laughs. I like to hear her laugh.

After another minute, she says, "So. Did you finally figure out why you run?"

Pop talked to her?

"Pop told me about your talk," she says, answering a question I didn't ask out loud.

Of course he did.

"He was worried about you," Mom says. "I worry about you."

"I did a lot of thinking," I say. "I had a lot of things I needed to figure out."

"Don't we all," Mom says.

The road hums between us.

"You know, if you ever need to talk to someone, I'm here," Mom says.

"I know."

"That goes for you too, Amelia." Mom glances at Amelia in the rearview mirror.

"I know, Mom," Amelia says.

"I know I work a lot. But I have time for my daughters. Always."

The words make my throat ache. I'm glad Mom has time for her daughters. But what about Dad?

I don't mean to blurt out "I just don't want to be forgettable." But some things are too big to keep inside.

"What?" Mom glances at me. We're almost home. I wish I could have kept my mouth shut for a few more minutes. I don't feel like explaining what I mean.

But maybe it's time.

"I don't want to be forgettable," I say again.

"What makes you think you're forgettable?" Mom says.

"Because Dad forgot me. Us. Me and Amelia."

Mom sighs and shakes her head. "He didn't forget you, Leta. Some people don't know how to be what others need them to be. Dads. Partners. Friends."

I think about Sabrina, but only for a minute. My thoughts always seem to return to Dad.

"But that has nothing to do with you, Leta," Mom says. "You are one of the strongest, fiercest, kindest, most brilliant people I know. You are *not* forgettable. Ever."

My eyes blur. I blink hard.

"No one can forget your smelly shoes, anyway," Amelia says. Which makes me laugh so hard a snot rocket shoots out my nose.

"Oh, gross!" Mom says. Which makes me laugh even harder. And Amelia, too. And Mom, who adds a choppy "You're cleaning that off the dashboard when we get home."

We laugh until she swings into the driveway and parks the car under a waving-good-bye sky and a pale moon that smiles too.

Before we get out of the car, Mom says, "We're not the first young women who have been through what we're going through, you know. There are all kinds of women and all kinds of stories."

"Coach Mac told us something like that," I say. "She said other women have run our race before we ever did, and they stand with us on the starting line, and they run with us every step of the way."

Mom nods. "That's exactly right."

"So we're not the first girls who have been left behind," I say, glancing at Amelia in the back seat. She acts like she's not listening, but I know she is.

"Not even close," Mom says.

"And you're not the first woman who's had to figure out how to raise kids alone."

"No. I'm not." Mom smiles. It's sad, but it's genuine, too. "We all have our individual journeys, but we all share a journey too."

I think about that. I think that's the sisterhood. I think maybe it's already here. I don't have to do anything to build it, it's been here for hundreds of years already. And maybe girls like Brooke and Briana and Sabrina eventually recognize the power of the sisterhood, and when they do, they'll be welcome too.

"We're all welcome in the sisterhood," I say out loud, even though it's not *exactly* what Mom and I were talking about. "We all belong."

Mom looks at me until my cheeks get a little warm. "How'd you get so smart?" she says.

"I think that's probably your fault."

Mom laughs. "Let's go have dinner."

"Finally!" Amelia huffs from the back seat.

Even hangry little sisters are welcome in the sisterhood.

I take a sheet of printer paper and spread out my colored pencils on the table. I'm no artist, but sometimes I doodle.

So I doodle. I make myself a sign. Several signs. One after another.

I'll stick them on my walls. I'll tape them to my notebooks. I'll pin one to my track uniform. I'll carry it everywhere.

I've finished coloring one before Amelia wanders over to the table. "What's that?" she says. She loves to color. I'm actually surprised it took her this long to see what I was doing. She probably wants me to invite her to help.

"Something I need to remember." I slide one of the signs to her. "Made one for you, too."

I didn't actually make one for her, but this is a sisterhood, and I can share. And the words are just as true for her.

"Unforgettable," she says and tilts her head at me. "What's it mean?"

"It means you're unforgettable," I say. "And so am I."

Amelia traces the letters. "Unforgettable," she says again. "The unforgettable Amelia Laurel."

"That's right."

"And you're the unforgettable Leta Laurel."

"And we're the unforgettable Laurel sisters."

Amelia grins at me before looking back down at the sign. She doesn't even wait a minute to say, "I could have colored this way better."

She's not wrong, but I still feel offended. "I was in a hurry," I say. "Be grateful for what you get" is what I really want to say.

"I'm gonna redo it," she says, and she takes three pieces of printer paper from me. I've already outlined the letters. Four unforgettables on one page.

She does color them way better than me, so I let her.

"There," she says when she's finished them all. "Now they're pretty."

My first sign, the one I colored, sits front and center on the table. "Mine was pretty too." We both sit there staring at it. But it's not pretty. It looks like a kindergartner scribbled a little color on some puffy letters. I wrinkle my nose.

"We all have our talents," Amelia says. "Not everybody can be good at coloring."

"Not everybody can be good at running," I say. Amelia's terrible at running. She complains about having to run a lap around her elementary school, which isn't even a full lap around a track.

She shrugs like she doesn't care one bit. She doesn't want to be good at running. I shouldn't want to be good at coloring—because no one can be the best at everything, right?

I know this is a sisterhood, but I still don't like it when my little sister proves she's wiser than me.

Fifty-one

THURSDAY

Mom takes me to a doctor. Pop said he'd pay for it and insisted I go. He says he's glad I figured out why I run, but he doesn't want me running on a damaged foot. And sitting out could be part of my journey.

I don't want to sit out. But I understand, sort of. Running isn't what makes me unforgettable; I am. Just me. Just Leta.

Also, the body is weird. And I know running on something that's already damaged can cause even more damage, and I don't want to risk never running again just so I can run one race that's over in a little more than sixty seconds.

The doctor, a tall man who runs long distances I can't even imagine, like Pop, takes an X-ray. He says there's no break or fracture, but my pain is a stress response. My body's way of warning me *before* it breaks or fractures.

"Rest will do you good," he says. "You don't race again for how long?"

"Nine days," I say.

He nods. "And you're doing pool running?" he says.

"My feet never touch the ground," I say. "My coach won't allow it."

"Good for her," he says. I like that he assumed my coach is a woman. Not everyone does. "Well, if you keep doing what you're doing, I'd say you'll be ready for your race."

Mom thanks him, and we head out to the car.

"Well, that was good news," Mom says.

"With a huge price tag," I say.

"You don't have to worry about that, Leta," Mom says. "It's not your responsibility."

But I don't want to cost too much for her or for Pop. We barely have enough money for food, much less stupid track-related injuries.

Mom sighs. "Listen, Leta. It's true that money's tight. But I'm getting help. And one thing I can tell you after all these years is that things always seem to work out."

It's true. They do.

"I worry about money a lot," Mom says. "And I'm sorry you've had to see that." I'm about to tell her she doesn't have to apologize when she says, "But we somehow always have enough. Even for good news at doctors' offices." She bumps my shoulder. "*Especially* for good news at doctors' offices. Who wants bad news?"

True again.

"One day at a time," Mom says.

It sounds like running advice. *One step at a time. One curve at a time. One day at a time.*

That's how we run our race.

Fifty-two

FRIDAY

On Friday I turn in my letter assignment. Eight letters to four important people in my life, not five like Mrs. Crisp told us. One for Mom (someone I admire), one for Pop (someone I love), one for Natalie (someone I'd like to know better), five for Dad (someone who hurt you *and* someone who meant a lot but isn't around anymore—I thought Mrs. Crisp would understand that I chose Dad for both of those categories). I added one for Coach Mac (another someone I admire) and one for Amelia (someone I love). I didn't want Amelia to feel left out. Not that I'll ever show her my letter.

Mrs. Crisp smiled at me when I handed her the folder, which was probably a little thicker than necessary. Some of those letters required two or more pages to say what I needed to say. Dad's five letters were a whole eight pages collectively.

"I knew you could do it," Mrs. Crisp says. "Can't wait to read them."

I feel lighter walking out of her classroom. Like I left all my worries and fears stacked neatly in a blue folder in Mrs. Crisp's hands.

Maybe I still carry things that need letting go. Maybe friendships won't get repaired, or boys will pick up their teasing again somewhere along the way, or injuries will come up every now and then, especially in the places you can't see.

Maybe it takes a long, long time to settle into the sisterhood. And maybe we take a long, long time to become our best.

But I think I'm on my way. I said what I needed to say. *I love you, I miss you, I forgive you.*

Natalie's back with us at lunch today.

"Where'd you go the last few days?" Raina says.

"Yeah, we missed you," Chrissy says.

And I realize we really *did* miss her. I start to tell her the same when she says, "I was working on my letter project for ELA. I had a little trouble getting started."

"Tell me about it," I say. I don't mean to. But there's

something about Natalie that makes me want to share.

She looks at me with her big brown eyes. "You too?"

"Yeah." I glance at Chrissy and Raina. "I was trying to write some letters to my dad, but I didn't even know where to start."

"Same," Natalie says. "What do you say to a person who leaves you?"

We look at each other, and I see myself in her. I bet she sees herself in me.

"Well, I wrote one of my letters to my mom," Raina says. "And I told her the truth. That I hate her for leaving me but also love her because she's my mom." She pops a Cheetos puff in her mouth. "I mean, I said a lot more than that, because it had to be at least a page. But that was the most important part."

Huh. I guess I could've started by telling the truth. If I'd actually asked my friends about it, I would've learned this sooner.

Natalie turns to Chrissy and Raina. She says, "I'm so glad y'all invited me to sit with you."

Before anyone else can say it, I say, "We're glad you're here."

Natalie's smile lights her whole face.

After lunch I catch Natalie's arm. I say, "You don't have to apologize for winning, you know."

Natalie says, "I could tell it meant a lot to you, though."

"I didn't run that race for the right reasons," I say. "I wanted to bring my dad back home."

Natalie drops her eyes to the ground. "Yeah, well, if you had asked me, I could tell you that never works."

"I know."

"But running does help you with the disappointment of it not working," Natalie says. She smiles as she says it.

"I'm starting to understand that," I say.

She nods.

"I'm really glad we're friends," I say.

"Me too," Natalie says.

"Not just friends. Sisters."

Natalie laughs. "I would say I already have enough of those. But I don't think you can ever have enough sisters."

I shrug. "We're a sisterhood, right? We look out for each other. We belong to each other."

"We run our race together," Natalie says.

And that sounds much better than running it alone.

Fifty-three

A FUTURE SATURDAY

I've waited practically all day to run this race.

Two heats, one final.

Here we are.

Natalie's in lane two; I'm in lane four. Not my favorite place to be, but really, I'm just glad to be here.

This morning I packed my old shoes in my backpack, not sure if I'd want to wear them today instead of the shiny bright ones Pop got me, for reasons I can't fully explain except to say that they're familiar, and there's comfort in the familiar. In the end, I decided to lace up the new ones.

Bright, like my future.

"On your mark."

I check my feet, ready my muscles, and clear my mind.

I close my eyes and imagine all the women who have run this race before, standing behind me, ready to cheer me on to the finish.

"Get set."

One quick look at the stands. All the important people are here: Mom, Pop, Amelia. I don't go looking for anyone else.

I won't dwell on the empty seat.

You are the unforgettable Leta Laurel, I tell myself. *You run to be free.*

The gun blasts, and I explode from the blocks.

I head for the first curve. I run harder than I've ever run, and my foot lets me. I fly.

Not for him.

For all the women who have come before and all who will come after.

And for me.

Author's Note

Once upon a time, girls weren't allowed to play sports. But on June 23, 1972, Title IX of the Education Amendments of 1972 was signed into law by President Richard Nixon. Title IX allowed girls and women to participate in sports and other federally funded educational programs and activities. Rep. Patsy Mink wrote the bill, with significant contributions from Rep. Edith Green and Sen. Birch Bayh.

As a result of Title IX, many schools began funding women's sports programs and, for the first time, colleges offered scholarships to women athletes.

Title IX had a long way to go—and a whole lot of opposition.

The deadline for high schools and colleges to comply with Title IX regulations was July 21, 1978. But even today, we're still finding our way.

When I was a young woman in the 1990s, competing in middle school volleyball, basketball, track and field, softball, and tennis, I didn't think much about Title IX. I took it for granted that women had always been allowed to play sports; by then about 1.9 million female high school students participated in sports. Today the numbers are even greater—but boys still have around 1.3 million more opportunities to play high school sports than girls have, according to the Women's Sports Foundation. Girls' sports at every level—middle school, high school, college, professional—still receive less funding than boys' sports. Women athletes—professional, amateur, and everything in between—are still fighting for equal pay, equal treatment, and equal rights.

It's not fair. Still.

Add to that unfairness improper education about our bodies.

In this book, main character Leta Laurel has to navigate her period during a competitive season in track. She has a supportive coach and effective period education—and she is in the minority. A 2021 study suggested that only

8 percent of elite female endurance athletes felt like they had sufficient knowledge about how their periods affect their performance and training. About 81 percent of their coaches—who were mostly men—lacked knowledge.

Without proper period education, those who menstruate can't understand their bodies and the markers they should look for to protect against overtraining and underfueling—something many female runners struggle with.

I'd had almost no period education and had no idea how to use my cycle to best accommodate and maximize my training when I was competitive in track. Thanks to Dr. Stacy T. Sims, an exercise physiologist and nutrition scientist, I now know more than I used to. Look her up if you want to know more about how to train for sports with a period. (https://www.drstacysims.com/)

Runners—especially female runners—often believe the myth that lighter is faster. This leads them to restrict calories and the food their body needs, which can lead to energy deficiency, which can turn into bigger problems like injuries and holes in bones if they continue restricting calories.

When I was Leta's age, I fell for the myth. I struggled (and still struggle during difficult periods of my life) with disordered eating for a very long time—though there were other reasons for my restriction, which was well on its way to becoming an eating disorder. Maybe I'll write about that someday.

My disordered eating *did* lead to energy deficiency. And though my running story ended a little differently than Leta's (I was district champion in the four-hundred-meter dash), I nursed injuries because of my calorie restriction.

The body needs fuel to perform its best. Remember that. (So does the brain, by the way.)

Lastly, middle school is an emotionally charged time of big feelings and changing loyalties and friendships and bodies that feel different every day. All that can make us feel insecure and anxious.

When we go through difficult times on top of that—parents divorcing, a father leaving, a mom struggling to put food on the table—we can forget who we are. I did.

My mom worked two jobs, sometimes three, all throughout my middle school years. My dad wasn't in the picture. I had to care for my siblings when I was just a kid myself. My giant emotions were eating me up inside—sadness and disappointment and jealousy for what my friends had that I didn't have. I lashed out at a friend. I apologized years later, but I still feel badly about that time. I did not uphold the sisterhood.

I do now. And you can too.

What is a sisterhood? It's a collection of people who work for the good of their sisters. They come to each other's defenses and they protect and they unite and they make sure everyone is treated with the dignity and respect and love they deserve.

And guess what? Everyone is a sister.

Why do we need a sisterhood? Because, as I mentioned before, the world is still not equal for women—definitely not in female sports. Sisterhood is the way we stand against inequality, the unfair treatment of women and other marginalized people, those demeaning "lists" made public (like in this story) or kept secret. There is strength in numbers, and a sisterhood stands together and says, "We are more than our bodies and other people's judgments." A sisterhood helps us remember who we are when we forget.

To uphold a sisterhood isn't easy or simple. It takes bravery and conviction and resolve and persistence and a heart that is both soft and strong.

As you navigate this tricky time, hold tight to the sisterhood. Honor each other. Love each other well. We need everyone—boys and men, girls and women, and everyone in between—to stand with the sisterhood and say, "We are in this together. We all deserve a spot at the table. To be safe and secure and loved and accepted for who we are."

We are not in competition for limited resources. That's a lie we were told to keep us small. There is enough to go around. And everyone belongs.

"When humans are ranked instead of linked, everyone loses," Gloria Steinem wrote in *My Life on the Road*.

Sisterhoods link.

Everyone is a sister.

Let's show the world what we're made of.

Acknowledgments

Every book is a study in sisterhoods. There are so many people who supported me, lifted me up when I was down in the dumps, talked me out of giving up, provided me with important information, and helped me shape this book into the one you hold in your hands. I am so grateful to:

Ben—for listening, sometimes endlessly, to my wild ideas and hopes. And for cooking us dinner so we all stay alive. Thank you for believing in me and joining me in this roller coaster of a life, wholeheartedly. I love you always.

My favorite boys—for being the first readers of this story. Thank you for your insightful (and sometimes silly) questions, for laughing in all the right places, for always listening and being readers and just... being your magnificent selves. I'm so glad I get to be your mom. But seriously. Stop growing up so fast!

My fellow Zoombies—for the constant encouragement and camaraderie. Special thanks to Anne for reading an early draft and telling me every thing that was wrong and a few things that were right. Thank you for your friendship and for always challenging me to be exactly who I am. What a sisterhood we belong to.

My own Coach Mac—for showing me I had the potential to win big. Without you, I wouldn't have. Thank you for believing in me and telling me like it was—I was talented, but I had to work hard. And no one could hold me back except myself.

Mitzi Lancaster—for, first of all, returning probably the weirdest phone call ever and, second of all, answering questions about what girls' middle school track practices and meets look like today. Any mistakes and errors are my own.

Dr. Stacy T. Sims—for all the research you've done on female athletes and menstrual cycles. I'm so glad I discovered your work and could finally make sense of my body's natural rhythms and adjust my endurance training to it. I hope a new generation of young women discover your research.

Diane Rosenfeld—for your research on the bonobos

and for giving modern women a vision for what the sisterhood could and should be.

All my sisters in the sisterhood—We're all in this together. Onward.

Rena—for always believing in me and my work and trying valiantly to balance all my many writing interests. I don't know if I can ever say enough thank-yous to capture the depth of my gratitude.

Kara—for not only believing in this story but also for helping me shape it into something beautiful and important. Thank you for being open-minded and supportive and for constantly reminding me that my stories matter. I'm so glad to have you in my sisterhood.

Dion MBD and Laura DiSiena—for a gorgeous cover that captures Leta in her element—brave, focused, and determined to show the world who she is.

The team at Simon and Schuster, including Valerie Garfield, Anna Jarzab, Kristin Gilson, Olivia Ritchie, Sara Berko, Christina Pecorale, Emily Hutton, and the many other hands that touched this book and worked on it—for believing in this book and ushering it out into the world and supporting authors as though they're . . . well, sisters.

Booksellers, teachers, librarians—for getting this book into the right readers' hands, for reading my stories to your classrooms, for recommending and talking about them. Writers are nothing without you. Thank you for being a part of the sisterhood.

And you, my dear reader—for picking up this book. I hope you've found a little piece of yourself in these pages. And remember: We all belong in the sisterhood, no matter who we are. You belong, you are loved, and you are always, always enough.

About the Author

R.L. TOALSON grew up running wild through corn rows and cow-grazing fields and recording true and wildly exaggerated false tales to entertain her friends, family members, and anyone who would listen. She still runs (literally) wild through the streets of her city and spends most of her days recording true (if a little exaggerated) and false tales to entertain anyone who will listen. She lives in San Antonio, Texas, with her one brilliant husband, six delightful children, and two arrogant cats. She's the author of *The Colors of the Rain*, which won the Arnold Adoff Poetry Honor Award for New Voices in 2020; *The Woods*; *The First Magnificent Summer*; and *Something Maybe Magnificent*. Visit her at racheltoalson.com.